I0582000

ALIZA IN NAZI-LAND

ELYSE HOFFMAN

Copyright © 2025 by Elyse Hoffman
All rights reserved. No part of this book may be reproduced or used in any manner without written permission of the copyright owner except for the use of quotations in a book review. For more information, address: elysehoffman.com

ISBN (ebook): 978-1-952742-37-8
ISBN (paperback): 978-1-952742-38-5
ISBN (hardcover): 978-1-952742-39-2

Project 613 Publishing
elysehoffman.com

To my grandfather David,
my grandmother Shirley,
my mother Lydia,
my father Richard,
my sister Liana,
and to God, Who makes all stories.

While "*Aliza in Nazi-Land*" can be enjoyed as a standalone story, it is also a continuation of Elyse Hoffman's previous book, **The Hangman's Master.** Characters and plot details from **The Hangman's Master** might be referenced in this book.

You might enjoy this story more if you read **The Hangman's Master** first.

Thank you, and enjoy!

ELYSE HOFFMAN
The
Hangman's
Master

Prologue

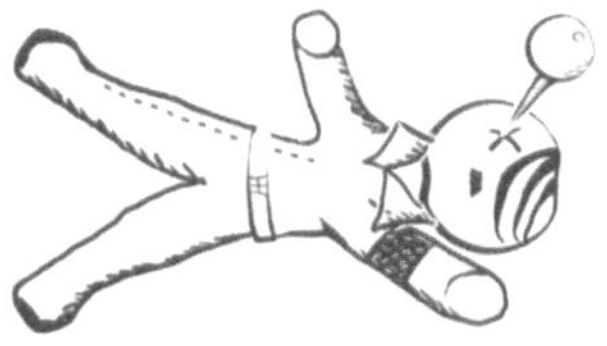

1945

Adolf Hitler had not expected to wake up after he put a bullet in his brain. The ever-arrogant Führer wasn't one to second-guess himself, and he had decided long ago that fanciful Christian notions of the afterlife were a scam at best and a childish superstition at worst.

So he hadn't expected to open his eyes and find himself in a bright white room after he pulled the trigger. And...well, Hitler hadn't even let the idea cross his mind that upon waking up in said room, he would rise to his feet and find himself facing a person sitting at a cluttered desk. A person wearing strange apparel: a grey cloak, grey gloves and a curved reflective mask that rendered them faceless.

He certainly hadn't expected that the oddly-dressed woman would toss confetti at him and toot a party horn before he could even consider getting a word out.

"Congratulations, you're dead," the person—a

woman, judging by her voice—declared with all the enthusiasm of a grade-school teacher that had lost her passion a decade ago. "You have lived a long and fruitful life of…"

The woman glanced at a clipboard before her and somehow managed to read the words on the paper even though her mask must have rendered her blind. "Fifty-six human years."

"I…what is going on?" Hitler sputtered, wiping the confetti off his dusty, torn up uniform and pressing a hand to the side of his head. He didn't feel a hole in his skull even though he had shot himself mere seconds ago. He ran his tongue along his crooked teeth and shivered because he could still taste the bitter-almond residue left behind by the cyanide pill. The deceased Führer could still feel the fading warmth of his wife nestling in his lap after she had bitten her own poison pill.

Eva, yes. Where was Eva Hitler née Braun? The loyal girl had killed herself so that she could be with Hitler in death, and yet the former Führer did not see his new wife anywhere. When he glanced about, he found that aside from the masked woman at the desk, there were only two other figures in the room: a duo of child-sized guards bedecked in red cloaks and mirror masks stood on either side of the white room's only door, a door decorated with two golden triangles, one which pointed up and the other pointing down.

"We understand that you are concerned about the state of your eternal soul," the woman at the desk said blandly, drawing Hitler's attention away from the door and back to her. "Your emotional state is very important to us, Soul Number 191-2455620435597, aka…"

She stopped and looked up, offering Hitler a view of his own scowling, distorted reflection for a brief moment before that reflection was rapidly replaced by different images: buildings on fire, planes dropping bombs, hordes of people marching behind barbed wire.

"Oh. Adolf Hitler," the angel said, and Hitler's reflection returned to the mask, no longer scowling but wide-eyed and trembling with fear.

The angel spoke in the same sort of tone that Hitler's older sister had once used when he pulled her hair and she knew that their father would beat his hide for that sin: "You are *damned.*"

▽

Chapter
ONE

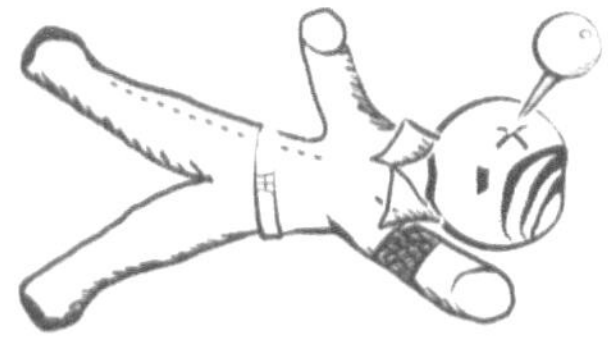

Aliza Auman couldn't remember her mother's face.

The sixteen-year-old girl was no amnesiac. She could remember a phone number just fine after hearing it a few times, and she had managed to cling to her reputation as a perfectly mediocre student in part because she could cram on the fly, stuff some information into her skull and remember it a day later. She wasn't a forgetful girl, but she couldn't remember her mother's face. In fact, she barely remembered anything from her early childhood.

This was forgivable, for Aliza Auman's childhood had been cut criminally short. Thanks to Hitler, and Himmler, and Heydrich, and all the rest of the monsters who made up the Third Reich.

Sometimes, she would remember little fragments. Not memories, not really, just sounds, smells, and feelings. A man's laugher as someone tickled her stomach and how much it hurt and how much she laughed. A gentle woman's voice whispering prayers in Hebrew. The soft heat of candles from…Hannukah, or Sabbath, something, *something…*

Those little memory ghosts would taunt her, tease her, and fill her heart with sorrow. She shouldn't have forgotten them; no girl should have simply forgotten her own parents. She wanted so badly to remember them, but she *couldn't.*

Because of Hitler, and because of the Fox Farm. Aliza despised that her earliest clear memories came from such an awful place.

Aliza didn't know how she had ended up at the Fox Farm, a pet project of Gestapo Chief Reinhard Heydrich. The Fox Farm had been a concentration camp specifically made to hold members of the Black Foxes, an anti-Nazi resistance group that had operated during the war. She could only assume that her parents had been Black Foxes too, or maybe a Black Fox had been trying to help her family only for all of them to be captured by the Nazis.

It didn't matter how much she would sit and strain her mind and try to remember. The questions were many, but all without answer. *Why were we there? What did she look like? What happened to them?*

Aliza hated that she couldn't remember them. She didn't even remember how they had died. Her earliest memory was being five years old, standing in the middle of a filthy barrack, utterly alone and utterly powerless.

Aliza hated that she couldn't remember her mother's face, no matter how much she cried and called out for her in her mind, but she could remember that feeling of helplessness so perfectly. She could summon it with hardly any effort.

She hated that. And that was how it always went: curiosity first, when she thought she heard a voice or felt something that reminded her of her first family. Desperation came next when she reached for them, stretching her mind into the darkness and fighting against the void, trying to find them. Then, sorrow consumed her when the only memories that surfaced were Nazis. Nazis screaming at her, Nazis kicking her stomach, Nazis killing someone right in front of her.

And then, after sorrow, hate. Hate because she couldn't remember her mother's face or her father's face, but she remembered the faces of the men who had taken them away. She knew the faces of the Nazis. She remembered Reinhard Heydrich's face from when he had visited the camp. Nobody would ever forget Hitler's face.

And so every morning began the same way for Aliza Auman: her sister Heidi would wake up before her, peek through the curtain that separated their sides of the room, and chipperly declare that she was going downstairs. Something about waking up and seeing a smile would summon the memory ghosts, and then Aliza would linger, sitting on her bed as the curiosity morphed and mutated into hate.

And then, once her heart was burning, Aliza would rise from her bed, stumble to her drawer, and pull out a souvenir from her final day at the Fox Farm. A dagger with a black hilt and a blade engraved in gothic writing: *Meine Ehre heißt True.*

She didn't remember her mother's face, but she remembered her last day at the Fox Farm. Not perfectly, there were still spots of cloudiness, but she remembered meeting her second father, Amos Auman, one of the Black Fox resistance fighters consigned to the camp. She remembered holding his hand while he told her that there was going to be an escape attempt and begged her to stay close. She remembered fire and smoke and gunshots. She remembered disobeying her new father for the very first time because Reinhard Heydrich had been inspecting the camp on the day of the break-out, and some morbid combination of fascination and hatred had driven her towards the man who had made her forget her mother.

The chief of the Gestapo had been preoccupied, she recalled, fighting with one of the Black Foxes. He had somehow been robbed of his gun and had been trying to stab the fighter with his ceremonial SS dagger, only for the dagger to be knocked out of his hand.

Aliza remembered the dagger landing at her feet. She remembered seeing her own reflection in the slightly bloodied dagger. She remembered being surprised by how long her hair was because she hadn't seen her own reflection in so long. She remembered picking the dagger up and feeling an odd sensation of power because she couldn't remember what her mother had looked like, but she remembered that her mama had never allowed her to touch sharp objects.

And Aliza remembered that she had wanted to run forward and stab her parents' murderer with his own blade, kill him with his own weapon because she knew that would sting him. But she remembered looking up, seeing his snarling face, and being too frightened because she was small and weak and *powerless.*

And then she remembered being dragged away from Heydrich and the Fox Farm. She had been whisked off to safety by Amos Auman and the rest of the Black Foxes and had spent the rest of the war in a Swiss orphanage.

Hitler had died. He had shot himself in the head when the war was nearing its finale. And Heydrich had died too, killed by Czech resistance fighters shortly after the Fox Farm was liberated. Himmler had chomped down on a cyanide pill. Goebbels had shot himself. Goering had poisoned himself before he could be executed by the Allies.

And it wasn't fair, because it wasn't enough. For making Aliza forget her parents, for stealing her first life, they should have all died worse. She would stand before the mirror and fantasize as she slashed at the air and envisioned herself giving them real justice, killing them all with their own tools, making them feel helpless and small…

"Aliza! Aliza Auman, if you don't get your butt to school, I'm letting Heidi paint your side of the room pink!"

And then, of course, her beloved father would shatter the illusion, and once again Aliza would become a powerless sixteen-year-old Holocaust survivor. And then she would sigh, bury the blade in her drawer, and try to force that horrible sinking feeling of helplessness to abandon her as she got dressed and attempted to focus on the good things she had. She was lucky, after all, even if she didn't feel lucky most mornings. She had a family, and a home, and her life, and that was more than could be said of most little Jewish girls that had spent time behind the barbed wire.

"*Aliza!*"

"Coming, Dad!" she cried as she ran a comb through her chin-length raven-black hair before throwing on a black undershirt and a black romper. Aliza did not remember her biological father, but luckily, she still had a dad.

Amos Auman smiled warmly at Aliza as she descended the staircase. During the war, Amos had served as a smuggler for the Black Foxes: he had shepherded the many orphaned Jewish children away from the Reich and to the safety of neutral nations. He, Aliza, and her sister Heidi had formed a bond in the Fox Farm and during their subsequent march across Europe. When Amos had dropped the girls off at the Swiss orphanage, he had vowed that once the war was over and he was done rescuing other children, he would return for them and give them a new home.

He had kept his word, and while Aliza would never forgive the Nazis for what they had taken from her, she couldn't complain about the life she had lived since the end of the war. Amos was a good father, and she certainly didn't lack family thanks to his finesse for adoption.

"Mornin', demon girl," Amos said, glancing down at Aliza's all-black outfit and offering a fond chortle. "Heidi set off without you. She didn't wanna be late."

"Miss Miller's always late anyway, I don't see the point of getting to school on time," Aliza said, pausing to glance at the Aumans' living room.

Amos wasn't a very materialistic man by nature, and he couldn't afford many toys for the girls, but she considered the place nicely furnished with all the familial necessities. There was a mantle decorated with a wax-coated menorah and a smattering of Russian dolls with expressions ranging from joy to shock that Aunt Ava had given them, souvenirs from her and her husband's time in the Soviet Union.

The walls were so thoroughly covered with the girls' drawings that Aliza didn't even remember what their wallpaper looked like. There was a TV which was so staticky that it wasn't worth watching most of the time and a radio that was missing a knob. A bookshelf stood against the wall, filled with comics and books about animals, and right next to that, there was a large wooden box with a heat lamp that served as their pet turtle Slowpoke's home.

And, of course, there was a secondhand couch that was serving as a balancing beam for a little girl.

"Morning, Shaina," Aliza greeted her sister.

"Shhh! Practicing!" the eleven-year-old squealed. Shaina was precariously balanced on the backrest of the couch, her arms outstretched, her tongue poking out of her mouth. Shaina had long sand-blonde hair that was always tied up in a bun and a burn mark on her face—she called it her lucky birthmark, and she was grateful that she didn't remember where she had gotten it.

Shaina didn't remember very much about the war except that at one point she had jumped or possibly been tossed from a train car and had managed a rather impressive landing-roll. She fancied herself an acrobat, partially because of that, and partially because her hero Aunt Ava had been a gymnast at one point.

Ever-indulgent Amos ushered Aliza out of the living room so as not to disturb the aspiring Olympic gymnast, yanking her into the dining room.

"Mornin', Liza," chirped the youngest Auman when she saw her sister. Uta Auman was ten, and unlike the rest of her adoptive family, she remembered absolutely nothing about the time before Amos had been her father, not even her original name. Amos and the Black Foxes had found a toddler wandering the woods, bleeding from a gash on her head, covered in mud, skeletally thin. When they had asked her what her name was, she had only replied, "Jew."

Amos had given her a proper name and a proper home, and Aliza was to this day not entirely sure if she pitied or was jealous of her sister for her utter amnesia.

At any rate, little Uta's scarred skull was now covered by a mess of curly black hair that was currently crowned by a ladybug headband. Uta loved animals (rather unfortunately, they had never been able to own anything bigger than a turtle since Amos, for one reason or another, was despised by every member of the animal kingdom. Even Slowpoke tried to bite poor Amos whenever he fed him.) Uta tended to switch the species she was obsessed with on a weekly basis, sometimes rotating back to old favorites.

Last week, she had been a leopard. This week, it was apparently ladybugs again.

"Morning, Uta. Eating aphids?" Aliza queried. Uta nodded, plopping an "aphid" (really, a green grape) into her mouth and chewing savagely. Aliza's stomach growled and she looked pleadingly at her father.

"Breakfast?" she said. Her father's lips tightened even as his smile didn't dissipate.

"Toast," he conceded.

"You're the best!" Aliza declared, scurrying into the nearby kitchen to prepare a scant breakfast. "No fair elementary opens later."

"Suits me just fine!" chirped Amos. It *would*, of course, since he happened to work at Uta and Shaina's elementary school. A good career for Amos, who loved kids enough that raising four daughters alone somehow didn't drive him absolutely insane. He wasn't a teacher quite yet, merely an assistant for the first-grade classes, but he would hopefully get his certification soon since he had finally become an American citizen after a long, arduous process some time ago.

Aliza, unfortunately, had to bear with teachers far less kindhearted than her father, and so she finished off her toast and grabbed her backpack.

"One minute, demon girl, you left this on the bay window last night," Amos said, shoving Aliza's world history textbook into her arms, his turquoise eyes twinkling teasingly. "And I have a feeling it went unread."

"I gotta B- last year…"

"I don't care what you make, hun. I *do* care that you try."

"Sorry, Dad," Aliza said with a small, genuine smile, hastily dumping the book into her satchel. "I'll study more after school."

She'd likely have no choice since the fact that she was

wearing a romper instead of a skirt was almost certainly going to arouse the anger of her gender-norm-enforcing teacher. Hopefully this time, she'd get a suspension instead of a mere detention.

"Atta girl," Amos said, giving her a brief hug. "Hey, when it comes to history, you might like it if you really *get into it.*"

"What?" Aliza chuckled as she pulled away, but Amos glanced at his watch and tapped its face.

"Late, late, for a very important date!" he teased. "Queen Miller will have your head!"

"Errr, right! See you tonight, love you!"

"Be home in time to clean Slowpoke's cage and do the dishes, don't leave it for your sisters *again!*" Amos cried as Aliza dashed out the door. "And tell Heidi the same!"

Aliza promised to be home on time, a promise that she was unlikely to keep, but she knew her dad well enough to know that he would forgive easily as long as she took on some other chore. It was Shaina's wrath she'd have to worry about if she made her do the dishes for the sixth night in a row.

Hastily, Aliza scurried into the streets of Beth-Hadasha. The Auman residence had the nicest front yard thanks to Amos and Heidi's shared love of gardening (Aliza liked gardening too, but only the digging in the dirt part, not the growing pretty flowers or useful veggies part.)

Quite a few of their neighbors' houses had over-grown lawns and cracked windows. This was to be expected. Beth-Hadasha had always been small, and it had always been Jewish (the synagogue still boasted a plaque commemorating when George Washington himself had taken refuge in the *shul* on a snowy Saturday morning after getting lost on his way to New York.) Since the end of the war, however, the little village had received a flood of new residents: Holocaust survivors, eager to leave their bloodstained homelands and find a new sanctuary, a new home amongst their own people.

They were good citizens, but they did tend to neglect material things. Houses, gardens, cars. That was understandable. They had all once had homes, and those homes had been stolen from them and transferred to their families' murderers. They all avoided getting too attached to any object, knowing how quickly it could be stolen.

Aliza winced as the loudspeakers spread about Beth-Hadasha crackled to life. A young woman's voice echoed across the small town: "Goood morning, Beth-Hadasha! It's a beautiful day in the U-S-A!" The loudspeakers were really meant to be reserved for emergencies: hurricanes or a nuclear bomb dropping on their heads. The citizens of Beth-Hadasha, however, had decided that if they were going to have a village-wide PA system, they might as well use it every day for more positive, banal messages. News about the local soccer team, the weather, announcements from the Rabbi…

"Oy, oy, oy! Damn pieces of garbage!"

Speaking of whom…

Aliza paused her journey to school and glanced across the street, her eyes landing on the Beth-Hadasha synagogue There was Rabbi Eliezer, spewing forth a string of curses certainly not suitable for a holy man as he stood in front of the plaque which commemorated George Washington's visit. Curious and concerned, Aliza quickly crossed the street.

"You okay, Rabbi Eliezer?" she said, and the old gentleman yelped in surprise before spinning around and greeting Aliza with a sigh of relief and a smile. Aliza felt her gut twist at seeing a few tears in his dark eyes: the Rabbi was always so nice to her, letting her wear a suit to synagogue services and rebuffing anyone who tried to make her leave and put on a "proper" dress. He certainly didn't deserve to be so upset.

"Ah, Aliza!" the Rabbi cried. "I'm all right, my dear, I'm all right! Just these damn posters."

"Posters?" repeated Aliza, stepping forward and peeking past the Rabbi's shoulder. Immediately, a familiar face made her seethe: a dark mop of hair, a square moustache, the face that she knew better than her own parents. The posters showed a drawing of Adolf Hitler shaking hands with George Washington. Right under that odd illustration was a picture of a bald, portly man with a smirk that could have made a raccoon vomit in disgust. "Nicholas Jackson" was printed beneath the portrait, and under his smirking visage was a bold proclamation in Germanic font:

JEWS ARE _LIARS_
JEWS INVENT _FAKE HISTORY_
BLACK-SUN BROTHERHOOD, LED BY GRAND LEADER NICHOLAS JACKSON, WILL LEAD A PROTEST AGAINST JEW _ATROCITY PROPAGANDA_
MEMORIALIZING THE _REAL_ HOLOCAUST AGAINST _GERMANS_ (OVER _60 MILLION_ KILLED!) IN HAMBURG, DRESDEN, AND BRENNENBACH!
STOP THE _HOLOHOAX_ FROM SPREADING!
JOIN THE BLACK-SUN BROTHERHOOD'S PEACEFUL MARCH THROUGH BETH-HADASHA!

"Holo-hoax?" Aliza repeated, and the ridiculousness of the poster's claims might have rendered it funny if it weren't so infuriating. It wasn't bad enough for the Nazis to kill her family, to make her forget them. No, now they wanted to pretend that they hadn't even done so. That Aliza's mother had never died. That her suffering was nothing more than a ploy.

The Rabbi, whose arm was tattooed with a telltale number which spoke of a stint in Auschwitz, shivered and tore another poster off the synagogue. "Bad enough they're coming here…" he whispered. "They just *have* to rub it in our faces."

"Bastards," Aliza concurred. Rabbi Eliezer sighed and tore down another poster, crumpling it up and tossing it into a pile at his feet.

"Anger won't fix anything, I suppose," he said. "Nothing we can do about it."

Aliza couldn't suppress the bomb of fury that went off in her gut as she felt an overwhelming wave of helplessness taunt her again. The Rabbi was right: there was nothing anyone could do about it. The Jews of Beth-Hadasha had tried their best to stop the Black-Sun Brotherhood, a Neo-Nazi gang, from marching through their village and retraumatizing the Holocaust survivors living there.

But the legal battles had all ended in failure. The courts had decreed that the First Amendment applied even to speech as vile as that spewed by the Neo-Nazis. As long as the Black-Sun Brotherhood didn't touch the people or property of Beth-Hadasha, they were free to have their march.

Aliza scowled at the smug visage of Nicholas Jackson, then let her gaze flit to Adolf Hitler's face before she growled, grabbed a poster, tore it off the synagogue, and ripped it in two, wishing that she could do the same thing to both of them, to all Nazis.

"I appreciate the help, Aliza, but you really should be running to school," the Rabbi said, patting her shoulder. "Go on! I'll have the place cleaned up in no time!"

"You sure?"

"You don't get to play hooky for me, missy!"

"Can't blame me for trying," Aliza quipped, and that earned a chuckle from Rabbi Eliezer, which lifted her spirits a bit. The Rabbi shooed her off, and Aliza ran towards her schoolhouse, again trying to douse the anger in her soul with positive thoughts. Living in a town full of Jews had its detriments, of course, namely the fact that the Nazis knew where to find them, where to maximize Jewish misery.

On the other hand, at least there was camaraderie in being cornered like this. Everyone in town had the same experiences. It was better, perhaps, to have to deal with anti-Semitism as a single typhoon once in a blue moon rather than a drizzle every day.

"...ugly-ass Nazi!"

On the other hand...

Quickly, Aliza slipped through the front gate and into the schoolyard, swiftly spotting her sister.

Amos often teasingly called Aliza and Heidi twins, partially because they happened to be the same age, but additionally because they were utter and complete opposites. Heidi had long blonde hair and light blue eyes. Aliza had dark hair and dark eyes. She also had a darker aesthetic, always dressing in black and grey, which contrasted mightily with Heidi's fondness for pinks and reds. While Aliza was a proud tomboy, Heidi was an absolute princess. While Aliza was rough, Heidi was sweet. While nobody would ever mess with Aliza Auman, Heidi Auman was an easy target.

Heidi's current tormentor was her most consistent bully: Yonah Meckler, class idiot. The tallest, meanest boy in their year who never grew sick of teasing poor Heidi. His dark eyes barely peeked out from his mess of curly bangs, twinkling with mischief. His slightly scarred face was twisted in a sneer as he grabbed one of Heidi's long braids in one calloused hand and tugged.

"C'mon, Auman, say it!" he commanded while a few of his brainless friends guffawed and Aliza's worthless classmates either laughed or simply looked on. Aliza was wise enough to know that almost all of the children in town had been teased and gawked at by crowds of bystanders when they had been shipped off to the ghettos and camps. Apparently, however, her fellow Holocaust survivors were too dumb to connect the dots and not indulge in the same behavior as their old German neighbors.

"C'mon, say it! Say, 'Heil Hitler!'" Yonah demanded again, ruthlessly pulling on Heidi's hair. Aliza's sister wailed and writhed.

"No, I'm not gonna, I'm not a Nazi!" she cried, and Aliza felt a pang in her heart. Yonah wouldn't know it—only Aliza, Amos, and their uncle Sam were privy to the knowledge—but Heidi had a very good reason for being particularly sensitive to such teasing.

Heidi had been rescued from the Fox Farm with Aliza, and she had been imprisoned there for the strangest of reasons: her mother and sister had been working for the Black Foxes right under the nose of her father, an SS offi-cer. Before Heidi had been Heidi Auman, she had been Heidi Naden, the youngest child of SS Captain Viktor Naden, the Beast of Belorussia.

Viktor Naden had been an absolute monster: an *Einsatzgruppen* officer under Heydrich's command, one of the Nazis who conducted mass shooting operations against East European Jews. Naden and his men had marched through Poland and the Soviet Union, burning villages to the ground, killing entire towns full of Jews.

After Naden's wife had been arrested, however, Hitler had turned against him, sending him to die on the brutal

Eastern Front. Unfortunately, Hitler had never believed in showing mercy to anyone: he had killed Heidi's mother and sister, leaving the little girl to rot in the Fox Farm.

Aliza had found her in that awful place, sobbing her eyes out, and little Heidi had abandoned whatever anti-Semitism her father had taught her when the Jewish girl had given her fellow orphan a comforting embrace. They had been sisters since then, even before Amos had officially adopted them, and Aliza wasn't about to let some asshole hurt her little sister.

Aliza offered no warning. She simply marched past the mass of bystanders, curled her hand into a fist, and decked Yonah Meckler right in the face. The boy released Heidi and collapsed into the dirt.

"Ow, what the Hell?!" Yonah yelped, spitting blood and wincing when he lifted up his hand to touch his quickly swelling cheek. He looked up, and his unpunched cheek turned scarlet when he saw it was Aliza.

"Fuck off, Meckler," Aliza said, cracking her knuckles, and Yonah didn't need to be told twice. He mumbled something incoherent under his breath and scurried inside, tail tucked. His goons followed.

"Dyke," one of the boys sneered as he walked past, and Aliza made a move as though she was about to lunge at him. The boy let out a rather girlish squeal that made her classmates snicker (trained seals that they were. Aliza was pretty sure that if they'd been born in different bodies, they would have happily joined the Hitler Youth.) With the show over, the rest of the teenagers started streaming into the small schoolhouse, leaving the Auman sisters alone in the yard.

"You okay?" Aliza asked even though it was clear that the answer was *no*. She helped Heidi to her feet. The blonde girl hastily wiped her eyes and yanked out a compact mirror, hiccupping when she saw her mascara running.

"Oh...I look awful," Heidi whimpered.

"So what else is new?" teased Aliza, and that managed to force a smile onto Heidi's face. The blonde girl elbowed her sister in the gut.

"Can you come to the bathroom with me so I can wash this off?" Heidi said, glancing nervously at the schoolhouse, knowing full well that however tantalizing a bullying target she was, nobody would dare to touch her while Aliza was acting as her escort.

"Sure. Miller isn't here yet?"

"No sign of her. Maybe she finally died?"

"Be'ezrat Hashem."

That earned another giggle from Heidi: Amos wasn't particularly religious, though he did insist on taking them all to synagogue for the sake of preserving the faith, but their Uncle Samuel was absolutely devout. Aliza wasn't entirely sure how she felt about her faith, but she did like some of the stories from the Torah (especially the ones about war) and she did like to incorporate Hebrew into her everyday lexicon. She didn't remember much about her birth parents, but something about the sound of Hebrew made her think of them, made a warm sensation bubble in her chest.

Heidi had confessed more than once that ever since she had learned English, German tasted sour. Her birth tongue reminded her too much of the bad old days, reminded her of the fact that if not for Hitler's depravity, she and Aliza would have been enemies instead of sisters.

Thankfully, the Aumans were all fluent in English, and most of the German-Jews from Beth-Hadasha didn't like to hear German. Unless they were bullying the seemingly Aryan Heidi Auman, of course. Heidi, however, never broke even when Yonah tried to force her hand. She'd rather have her hair ripped out than say anything in German, much less *Heil Hitler.*

They didn't discuss Yonah while they were in the bathroom. Heidi re-applied her makeup, taking her sweet time as she did so.

"Y'know that gunk's made from animal shit, right?" Aliza said. She had no idea what makeup was made of, but whatever it was must have been gross. "And crushed-up bugs."

"If it was made of shit and crushed-up bugs, you'd wear it every day," teased Heidi, re-applying her mascara and smiling at her lovely reflection. Aliza snickered at that. True. When they were young, Aliza would jump into every mud pit and capture bugs because she had thought they were cool. She had fond memories of chasing Heidi around the yard with a massive caterpillar on a stick.

"Switch seats with me today," Aliza said as they walked towards their homeroom. "Yonah must be moody. If he says shit to you again, I'm gonna break his nose and he knows it."

"Thanks, Liza..." Heidi said with a small smile. Aliza patted her sister's shoulder and they walked into the classroom. Yonah was there, leaning back in his chair and pressing an ice pack he must have stolen from the nurse's office against his bruised cheek. Briefly, he smirked when he saw Heidi only to wince when Aliza gave him a venomous scowl. He buried his face deeper into the ice pack and turned from her as she stole Heidi's seat beside him, shielding her sister.

Miss Miller was tardier than expected—she stumbled into the classroom nearly fifteen minutes late muttering something about how her elderly cat had needed a trip to the vet. Miller was a sour old lady with pink glasses that accentuated the mistrusting squint she always wore. Her grey hair was groomed and plaited, and her long dress was wrinkle-free and covered in cat hair.

"Let's get through the prayers and pledge quick," Miss Miller declared, pointing to the American flag hanging proudly above the chalkboard before moving her arm to gesture towards a poster of the Ten Commandments hanging right beneath it.

Oh boy, here we go, Aliza thought, standing up with all of her classmates. Prayer time went by without incident: Aliza liked the sound of Hebrew and didn't mind using it to thank God for what she had—she blamed Hitler for what she had lost, not God. When the rest of the students placed their hands above their hearts and started reciting the pledge of allegiance, however, Aliza folded her arms behind her back and stared silently but respectfully at old glory.

Aliza had nothing against the flag, the pledge, or America. She certainly liked America more than Germany, America hadn't tried to kill her and her entire family (yet.) Nevertheless, while she liked America, she hated the pledge. She hated that it was mandatory, and she hated the concept of starting the day vowing unflinching loyalty to a mass of land. The entire ceremony reminded her too much of the gaggles of Hitler Youths raising up their hand to salute their own flag. Because of that, Aliza refused to salute, refused to say the pledge, and merely stood for it, which she figured showed enough respect.

Generally, she could fly under Miller's radar if the old crone was tired or busy worrying about her army of cats. Today was not one such day. As soon as the pledge ended, Miller's perpetually annoyed gaze fell upon Aliza.

"Miss Auman..."

"Yes?" both Heidi and Aliza said in unison, like they always did. Miller grunted.

"Aliza Auman, please remain standing. Heidi, sit."

Heidi did, and Aliza offered a smile at her teacher. She likely would have been much ruder to the old hag if not for Amos. He was willing to let Aliza get away with a lot, but she would get the dreaded *"I'm disappointed in you"* if she actually insulted a teacher. Besides, Aliza didn't want to harm her father's chances at obtaining a job by becoming a byword among the miniscule teaching community of Beth-Hadasha. Better to let Yonah continue to be every teacher's least favorite student. Rebellion with a polite smile was still a rebellion.

"You didn't say the pledge, *again*," Miller snapped, sitting at her desk, folding her wrinkled hands in front of her, and scowling over her pink eyeglasses.

"Ma'am, the First Amendment guarantees every American the right to freedom of speech, and as a proud American..." Aliza started, only to be cut off by a growl from the teacher.

"Don't pull that, Auman! The First Amendment doesn't give you the right to do whatever you want. And furthermore..." Her cold eyes flitted down to Aliza's legs, and Aliza was ever-so-tempted to say something crude, something that would get her expelled rather than the desired suspension.

"You've *once again* failed to adhere to the dress code," Miller said. "Young ladies are not supposed to wear pants."

"This is a *romper*, ma'am, not pants."

"You can't pull that nonsense again, Aliza!"

Good, good, she was getting really frustrated. Aliza offered her sweetest smile. "Ma'am, I'd be happy to go home and change..."

"Oh, no, not this again!" Miller cried, leaping to her feet and slamming her hands on the desk before her. "The last three times you pulled that, you never returned to class! You're lucky my ruler is out of commission!"

The dreaded ruler, reserved not for math but for corporal punishment. Yonah and a few of his friends had broken it into little bits after Miller had smacked their knuckles raw. Aliza was still finding inches and centimeters in the schoolyard.

"I *should* call in a conference with your father again, but that would be a waste of my time!" Miller declared, and Aliza nearly snickered. The past parent-teacher conferences between Amos and Miss Miller had ended with Miller fuming after Amos spent the hour gently defending his daughter. (Miller had nearly lost it when she'd complained about Aliza's hatred of dresses and skirts and Amos had cheerfully responded that "femininity can come in many forms!")

"As it were, you won't be going home early, or even on time!" Miller snapped. "Detention for an hour! Now take your seat!"

Damn. No suspension. Aliza plopped down into her wobbly little chair with a huff.

"I'll wait for you." Heidi whispered before she was hushed. Yonah wouldn't linger on school grounds after the bell rang, so Heidi would be fine sitting by the front gate while he rushed off to do whatever the Hell he did after school.

Aliza sighed and sunk down in her seat, listening to Miss Miller prattle on about this and that and *respect for authority*. The girl felt like she was being stepped on by a giant. She was *so* tired of being ordered around, of being small, of being *powerless*.

—————— ▽ ——————

Chapter
TWO

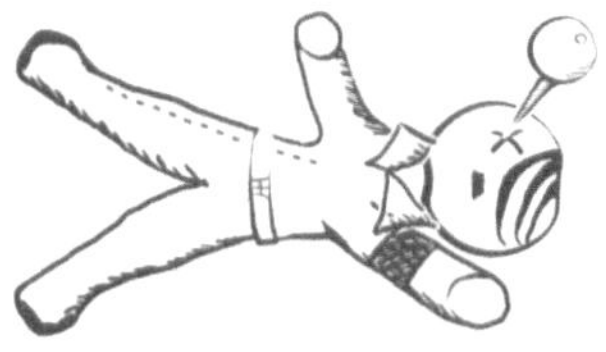

The rest of the school day trudged along at its usual snail's pace. English, then math, then science (the best class hands-down, especially because Mr. Schwartz always had some sort of dangerous chemistry set on hand that he was more than happy to let his students tinker with.) Eventually, mercifully, class ended. Heidi proclaimed that she'd be waiting on the bench outside, and Aliza, not wanting to test Miller too much, reported for detention.

"I'd assign you chalkboard writing," Miller said with a sigh, nudging her head towards the smudged onyx surface. "But you're behind anyway. Get your homework done. I'll be watching."

"Yes, ma'am," Aliza sighed, plopping down at her desk and taking out her pen and her hitherto unused history textbook.

As she did so, however, Aliza realized that something was different. There was a slight gap at the end of the book, as though something had been shoved inside to mark the space. Curiously, Aliza opened to the gap.

She winced as Hitler's scowl greeted her under Chapter 37. *"Modern History: America's Role in the Fight Against Fascism."* Tucked right under the chapter title, beneath the black and white picture of Adolf Hitler screaming at his minions, was a piece of sun-colored paper folded into a triangle. Aliza glanced up at her teacher, but fortunately, Miss Miller had ceased her blink-less vigil and was grading quizzes, only occasionally glancing up to make sure that the girl had her nose in her textbook.

Aliza touched the little triangle, wincing when her fingers brushed against it. It felt...warm. Almost like it was alive. Touching it reminded her of the time she had gone to a pet shop and touched a hamster: she could all but feel the thrum of a heartbeat.

Caution had never been something Aliza had possessed, however, and so she ignored a niggling sensation of dread that told her to ignore it and slowly unfolded the paper. Miller didn't notice.

It looked like some sort of legal document. At the top was an insignia: a yellow triangle inside a black circle with scarlet words written right beneath it: ***Hell is Mercy***. And right beneath that, in bold gothic letters, was a lyrical proclamation:

THE LORD HAS GIVEN THEE
A POWER KNOWN TO ONLY HE
THE POWER OF COMPLETE CONTROL
OVER THIS, A HUMAN SOUL
UNTIL THE MOMENT OF REPENTENCE
AND THE END OF THEIR SENTENCE
THE ONE WHO SIGNS THIS
CONTRACT
IS HEREBY THE MASTER OF
ZONE N-1

AND THE FOLLOWING SOULS CONFINED THEREIN:
Reinhard Tristan Eugen Heydrich
Adolfus "Adolf" Hitler
Paul Joseph Goebbels
Heinrich Luitpold Himmler
Hermann Wilhelm Goering

What the Hell...? Aliza thought, perhaps somewhat ironically. She might have dismissed this as some sort of practical joke if the paper laid out beside Hitler's face which proclaimed that it held the dictator's very soul didn't genuinely *feel* alive.

The pen in her hand felt heavy all of a sudden, and that dying little ember of dread counseled her against signing contracts that she didn't truly understand. But the empty signature line was too tempting, and even if it really was some sort of prank, it would be worth it for a chance that the paper would offer what it promised.

In one swift motion, Aliza signed the paper, and immediately, she felt a surge of something...power? This feeling was like nothing she had ever experienced before, helpless child that she was. The closest she had come to it was punching Heidi's bullies in the face. That sensation of strength, a rush, and then...nothing.

"Uh...okay?" Aliza muttered.

"Miss Auman, back to work!" snapped Miller, and Aliza sighed.

"Yes, ma'am," she said, and the teen fully intended on tucking the Contract back into the book and dismissing it all as a nonsense prank.

But as soon as she released the paper, it suddenly folded itself back into a tringle and flew right at her. She shrieked as the Contract planted itself right over her heart, pointing upside down. It didn't hurt, but confirmation of the Contract's magical status was certainly startling.

"Miss Auman, what is it?" Miller asked. She hadn't seen the Contract fly right at Aliza, then. *How?* Aliza wondered. *She was looking right at me...is it invisible?*

"Is your heart feeling okay?" Miller asked when she saw Aliza clutching her chest.

"I...I..." Aliza stuttered. It was a little surprising to see grouchy old Miss Miller look so genuinely concerned for anything except her army of cats, but then again, *bitchy* and *evil* were certainly not the same thing.

"Do you need me to call the nurse? Can you speak properly?" Miller inquired, rising to her feet as though she was prepared to help the girl to the nurse's office.

"I-I'm fine, ma'am, just a little start out of nowhere," Aliza said, and Miss Miller's eyes narrowed behind her pink glasses.

"All right," the teacher said in the gentlest tone that Aliza had ever heard from any of her teachers. "But get looked at by a doctor. Some genetic diseases don't start to appear until later, you know, and if it's something like epilepsy, you'll want to..."

But right then, it seemed that Miss Miller had some sort of episode herself. She stopped mid-speech, mouth agape, not moving, not even blinking.

"Miss Miller?" Aliza said, rising from her seat, ready to run to find the nurse for her teacher before she realized that Miss Miller wasn't the only thing that had become still. The American flag was no longer swaying in the slight breeze, perhaps because there *was* no breeze. When Aliza looked out the window, she saw squirrels frozen mid-jump as they leapt from branch to branch. Teens in the distance stood like statues. Time itself had stopped.

"My, my. And I was *just* about to send a scout to

retrieve the Contract to Zone N-1. All well and good: you were near the top of my list anyway."

A male voice, familiar and yet strange. A voice that she knew but couldn't fully remember. Aliza whirled around and found that she was not alone in this frozen moment in time.

A man—or at least she assumed that it was a man based on his voice—was sitting at a desk in the back row. Bedecked in a black cloak with an upside down yellow-tringle in the center of his chest. He wore black gloves, a black hood, and a strange mask that covered his face: a mask that appeared to be some sort of curved mirror, which reminded her quite a bit of the sort that she and Heidi would play in front of at the carnival when they were little.

"What the Hell?" Aliza said, and that fetched a chuckle from the oddly dressed stranger.

"You're right on the mark, Miss Auman. I suppose you realize now that the Contract wasn't bluster." The stranger gestured to the triangle stuck to her shirt. She gingerly touched the paper and then scowled at the masked man.

"You'll want an explanation and an introduction," the stranger said, rising from the little desk and strolling towards the window, idly glancing out at the motionless schoolyard like it was some sort of painting at an art gallery, even stroking the chin of his mirror mask as he did so. "I normally wouldn't rush, but your Contract is important, and it's been without a proper Master for far too long. Your predecessor decided that *he* should dictate how the Heavenly Host operates."

The stranger's voice took on a note of anger as he spoke, gloved hands curling into fists. "He crossed off his name without even bothering to find a proper replacement. Actually tried to *hide* the Contract and prevent anyone else from getting it. Ah, but I'm getting ahead of myself."

He turned around and uncurled his fists, crossing his arms over his chest and bowing towards the young girl. "My name is Ha-Satan."

A Christian girl in Aliza's shoes might have recoiled in horror upon realizing that she had signed a strange document and was now being approached by Satan himself. Uncle Samuel had taught Aliza about the many differences between Jewish and Christian theology regarding angels, however, and so she merely raised an eyebrow and said, "Ha-Satan the Heavenly Prosecutor?"

"Ah! It's so refreshing to not be called a demon!" Ha-Satan chuckled, sounding genuinely relieved as he straightened up and clapped his gloves hands together. "Saves me trouble and saves you panic. You're correct: I serve God the Almighty as his prosecuting attorney in the Court of Heaven. When you die, I will make note of your sins and bring them forth as evidence against you in Judgement. Don't take it personally, and don't fear. Most souls, after all, will only end up receiving short sentences in Purgatory. However, the few souls who have abused their free will, committed unspeakable crimes against mankind...men, for example, like *him*..."

Ha-Satan gestured to the textbook, to Hitler's scowling face. "These irredeemable souls will instead be given over to me. God has turned His gaze from them until the day that they truly repent of their sins and are freed from the pits of Hell. Until then, however, they must be punished, and the Lord, in His wisdom, has instructed me to oversee this punishment. Unfortunately, as an angel, I lack the creativity of humans. For some time, I simply left the sinful souls in the darkness of the Void. But then one day, a soul gave me inspiration."

Ha-Satan strolled towards one of the classroom bookshelves and plucked a well-worn paperback, holding it up to reveal that it was a copy of *Dante's Inferno*.

"Dante Alighieri," Ha-Satan declared. "Have you by chance read his masterpiece yet?"

"Yeah…" Aliza muttered. "Last year. The rings of Hell…boiling blood, frozen lakes…"

"Yes, yes!" the Archangel chirped with all the giddiness of a much younger Aliza Auman talking about the latest *Batman* comic. "Mr. Alighieri came up with the most wonderfully creative punishments, and who did he reserve them for? His enemies! This book is littered with scenes of Dante Alighieri's political and religious foes being tormented. His creativity is matched by his hatred. And so I thought: who better to give a sinner their just sentence than humans like Dante? Creative humans with a vendetta. And so, I devised the Contract system."

Ha-Satan set the book down on the desk in front of him and gestured to the Contract on Aliza's chest. "I select humans such as yourself and give them a small section of Hell, a Zone, which contains a certain number of dead sinners. For Hitler, typically, I choose a Jew to become his Master. As it were, you will make a perfect God of Nazi-Land. All's well that ends well."

"This…" Aliza muttered, tapping the Contract as she continued to feel it thrum and hum. "It feels alive."

"It is, in a way," Ha-Satan said. "That Contract holds the free will of the men listed, a part of their soul. By signing it, you have become their God. Merely think, 'I want to go to Zone N-1,' and your soul will be transported to the Zone which holds their souls, a universe where you have complete control. From there? It's up to you. You may do whatever you wish to your Subjects: simple brutality and torture, or a carefully concocted story to hit at their emotions and insecurities. If you truly wish, you may even exert your will onto your Subjects, give them a

Command which will force them to do or say whatever you wish. The possibilities are endless."

"This...is a dream," Aliza finally guessed, shaking her head and pinching her arm. "I must have fallen asleep in class."

"I don't blame you for thinking that, Miss Auman," Ha-Satan said with a small shrug. "However, when you wish, when you're comfortable, I invite you to see for yourself. Do be sure to only enter your Zone when you're in an environment where you won't be bothered: if someone disturbs your body while you're in the Zone, you'll be safely pulled out, but your fun would end too soon!"

Ha-Satan chuckled, offered her one final bow, and proclaimed, "I must continue with my duties. If you want to know anything else, I encourage you to read the manual provided in the Master Room. Good luck to you, Miss Auman!"

"Wait, Master Room, what—?"

"...have a lot of health problems...oh dear, you don't look too good. You can leave early, Aliza. Serve out the rest of your detention when you're feeling better."

But Aliza blinked, and the Archangel was gone. The world was moving again. The girl might have thought she'd merely had a psychotic break if she hadn't looked down at her chest and seen the Contract still glowing there. When she lifted her eyes, she saw that *Dante's Inferno* was sitting on top of the desk where Ha-Satan had left it.

"I...thank you, ma'am," Aliza stuttered, grabbing her textbook and offering a genuine smile at her teacher. "I'll head out."

Miss Miller's concern and kindness itself would have been enough to make Aliza think that she was dreaming, but even as she exited the classroom and scurried down the hall, pinching herself and ramming her skull against lockers when desperation set in, she didn't wake up.

*That was real, then...*Aliza thought, her mind buzzing as she brushed her fingers against the Contract. *All of that was real...*

Eagerness gripped her heart as fierce as it had when she was a child looking forward to gifts on the first night of Hannukah. Aliza had always been haunted by the concept that the Torah was a lie, that there was truly nothing after death. She despised the notion that her parents were completely gone, and equally, she despised the idea that her tormentors would go unpunished. Hitler deserved so much worse than a self-inflicted shot to the skull, and now it was up to Aliza to give him his dues.

That feeling of power flowed through Aliza Auman's body, and she all but bolted out the door, eager to get home. Ha-Satan had warned her to wait until she was in a safe locale to test out the Contract, and so she would have to get to her room and then, *then* she would *finally* get her revenge.

"...I was just hoping..."

"I'm sorry, sir, I really don't speak German."

Heidi's distressed voice pulled Aliza from her ruminations and excitement. Aliza scurried out of the schoolyard and found her sister sitting on the outdoor bench, her posture stiff and nervous as an older gentleman hovered above her, speaking in German. A new refugee, probably, if the moon-shaped scar cutting across his face and the fingers he was missing on one hand were anything to go by. Almost everyone in Beth-Hadasha had scars, visible or otherwise.

Still, he was clearly making Heidi upset, and so Aliza pushed her magical encounter into the back of her mind and rushed forward to protect her sister.

"...I...are you absolutely certain you can't...?" the man said, slowing his speech. Heidi bit her lip and squirmed but brightened when she saw Aliza.

"Hi, sis!" Heidi announced loudly, hopping up and all but leaping behind her sister. Aliza flashed a toothy smile at the stranger.

"*Hey, sir,*" Aliza said, switching to her native tongue. "*Did you need something?*"

The stranger's eyes flitted between the girls, widening. His eyes...light blue, very much like Heidi's, and that scar. Aliza felt her heart summersault and she reached out, grabbing her sister's arm, ready to run if her suspicion turned out to be correct.

"*I...*" the man stuttered, staring at Heidi a bit too long before bowing his head and quietly muttering, "*I was just wondering where the nearest bus stop is.*"

Aliza gritted her teeth. Either she was wrong, or Heidi's biological father had decided that he loved his child more than he hated Jews. "*Down Salomon Street, then take a left. Can't miss it. We have to go. Our dad is expecting us, and we're not supposed to talk to strange men.*"

"*Right...*" the stranger muttered. "*Good day to you, then, ladies...*"

He spared one final mournful glance at Heidi before setting off down the street, noticeably limping as he did so. The result of surviving the Nazis, or serving them on the East?

"Creep," Heidi said when the stranger finally vanished from sight. Aliza nodded slowly, and as she and Heidi set off for home, Aliza kept glancing over her shoulder.

"Thanks for saving my butt back there," Heidi said. "He was being *so* weird. I swear I've actually seen that guy around town sometimes, and he just *stares* at me. I think I'm gonna ask Uncle Sam if I can have that pocketknife after all."

"Yeah..."

"Something wrong?" Heidi queried, gazing at her sister with concern shining in her blue eyes. "Sorry, I was too focused on me, didn't even ask how detention went for you."

"Same as usual. Just…got to thinking about stuff…" Aliza muttered, glancing down at the Contract on her chest. Heidi hadn't noticed it at all, just like Miller hadn't, which likely meant that it was completely invisible to everyone except Aliza herself.

"Stuff like…?" Heidi prodded, and since she didn't much feel like getting hauled off to the nearest insane asylum, Aliza decided that it would be pertinent to keep the Contract and her encounter with an Archangel secret.

"Stuff like…the march…" Aliza lied.

"Oh, yeah…" Heidi muttered, glancing at the synagogue as they passed and giving a relieved sigh when she saw that all of the Black-Sun Brotherhood's posters had been torn down. "I saw that this morning. It's so terrible! After everything that everyone went through, and we're all just doing our best to move on."

"Move on…yeah…" muttered Aliza, glancing nervously over her shoulder. She was getting the eerie sense that she was being watched, which either meant that Ha-Satan was keeping an eye on her, or the stranger hadn't gone to Salomon Street.

"Hey, Heidi, I was wondering…" Aliza said, clutching at the Contract on her chest, curiosity and caution making her ask a question that she knew wouldn't have a comfortable answer. "Do you…remember your father at all?"

"Uh, yeah, I'm not *that* dumb," snickered Heidi, evidently unable to sense any stranger's presence as she grabbed her sister's arm and started wrenching her towards their cul-de-sac. "I remember he told me this morning that if we didn't have the dishes done…"

"No, Heidi," Aliza said, pulling her arm out of Heidi's grasp and giving a small sigh of annoyance. "I mean your *real* father."

Aliza truly hated asking: there was a silent agreement between the two of them that Heidi Naden had never existed. There was just Heidi Auman, Jewish girl, Holocaust survivor. Aliza had always wondered how much Heidi remembered of her life as a Nazi's daughter, however, and now it seemed that sating that curiosity could be important.

Immediately, Heidi's teasing smile morphed into a grimace. She looked down at her shoes, gripping the straps of her backpack so tight that her knuckles turned placid as she hissed, "Dad *is* my real father."

"Heidi, come on, I mean it," Aliza prodded, masking her slight aggravation at her sister's evasion with a soft note of sympathy. "Do you have any memories of...?"

"No, okay!? I don't!" Heidi snapped, finally looking up. Heidi was typically more wont to cry than actually get mad even in the worst of situations, and so it was rather startling to see her eyes blaze with fury. "My memories basically start the day that the Nazis arrested me and mom and my...my first sister."

Heidi paused, swallowed a lump in her throat, and let out a shuddering breath. They never talked about her father, and sometimes Heidi spoke about her mother when reverently declaring that she had been a brave Black Fox. Heidi's first sister, Nadine, however...Aliza only ever heard Heidi mention her when she cried out in her sleep.

"And then my clearest memory is watching the Nazis kill my mom and my sister and..." Anger was petering away into sorrow. The fire left Heidi's eyes, replaced by tears. Quickly, Aliza did as she had when they were little girls at the Fox Farm: she threw her arms around her sister, giving her a tight embrace which Heidi eagerly returned.

"And then there was you, and then there was Dad and Uncle Sam," Heidi hiccupped. "And that's *all.* I don't remember him at all, and I don't want to. Fuck him! The only good thing Hitler ever did was take me away from him! I am *not* a Nazi's kid, I am *not*! I'm a Jew, and I'm an Auman, and that's all. That's all I want…"

"All right. I'm sorry. I won't bring it up again, I was just…y'know, thinking about stuff…" Aliza said, releasing her sister and letting out a small sigh of relief when she felt the sensation of being watched fade away. Whatever had been observing the sisters must have left.

"Never mind. It doesn't matter," Aliza declared with a shrug. "C'mon, we've gotta get home or Dad's gonna get mad."

Heidi wiped at her tearstained cheeks and nodded, a shaky smile blooming on her face. "Dad doesn't get mad, Dad gets *disappointed*. Ah, shit, my makeup again!"

"Here." Aliza offered her dark sleeve to her sister and Heidi wiped her running mascara off on the romper.

"There," Aliza declared. "Now you're just a *little* less ugly."

"Ugh, you're such a jerk!" said Heidi in a tone that was at once a shriek and a laugh, smacking her sister in the arm and eliciting a cackle from Aliza.

"C'mon," Aliza said once Heidi had calmed down. "Let's get home so Shaina can murder us."

"Oh boy, can't wait to be murdered," Heidi sang. The two of them quickly returned to their home, noticing a bike parked in front of the dahlia garden.

"Uncle Sam's here!" Heidi squeaked. Amos' old friend from the Black Foxes, Samuel Val, was a dear family friend. Since his girlfriend had moved to DC for work a few weeks ago, Sam had been coming over more and more for dinner. "Eating alone is depressing," he had sighed. "Gotta have some family around."

Sam certainly didn't lack loving family whenever he visited the Aumans: Amos was only too happy to cook for his old friend; Uta was always happy whenever Samuel shared stories and fairytales from his *shtetl*; Shaina loved having an extra set of hands to applaud her gymnastic moves; and Heidi, whom Samuel spoiled like a princess, was always overjoyed to see their uncle.

As for Aliza, she and Sam shared a mutual love of comic books—she liked Batman, he preferred Superman, this was a point of great contention between them. Nevertheless, Sam always brought several editions of every comic book he could get his hands on whenever he visited, meaning that Aliza didn't have to dip into her own allowance to keep up with the marvelous adventures of her favorite superheroes.

Surely enough, when the sisters entered their living room, there was Samul resting on the couch and reading the latest issue of *Action Comics*. Samuel was a tall man with dark brown hair and striking bright blue eyes. Even when relaxing, he wore a frosty poker-face. Many people in Beth-Hadasha tended to assume that the seemingly ever-serious man had a hard heart. In reality, though, he was simply guarded and subtle in his love. When Heidi ran up to him, he tossed aside the comic book and embraced her, his miniscule smile failing to match the joy that shimmered in his eyes.

"Hey, *bubbeleh*, everything all right?" he asked. Heidi kissed Sam's cheek and nodded.

"I hope you young ladies have a very good explanation for why Shaina just did all of the dishes *and* fed the turtle!" Amos' voice echoed from the kitchen. Aliza and Heidi glanced at one another, but before either of them could fumble for an answer, Sam saved them.

"Lay off 'em, Amos!" he cried. "I asked them to deliver a package for me."

"Oooooh, a package, eh?" Amos snickered. "That

would be the sixth package this week! Who could possibly be getting all of these packages?"

Aliza cloyingly and annoyingly leaned close to her blushing uncle and sang, "Hanaaaa!" The scowl that she received for her troubles could have melted steel.

"I'm never saving you again," grumbled Samuel. Aliza giggled and kissed her uncle's cheek.

"You've gotta marry her, uncle," Heidi said, tossing her backpack aside before scurrying over to Slowpoke's cage and greeting the family pet by opening the lid of his enclosure, reaching in, and stroking his shell. "I wanna be someone's cousin!"

"You have Auntie Ava's son, Heidi!" cried Amos, and that made Heidi let out a loud gag.

"Otto's not a *cousin*," she announced. "He's a *disease*."

Aliza cackled at that and gave her sister a high-five. Sam sighed and rolled his eyes.

"Sam, you should invite Hana to come back home for Purim!" Amos shouted. "I'm sure it must be lonely in DC."

"She's with her uncle for Purim this year, and I'm too afraid of him to go anywhere near his house," Samuel said with a shrug and a slight grimace.

"You're a Black Fox!"

"*Ex* Black Fox," Samuel noted, and indeed, it did sometimes slip Aliza's mind that the Black Foxes were still in operation. Most of their agents that had fought during the Second World War had retired, but a few continued to serve, now trying their best to save those trapped behind the Iron Curtain. Stalin was no better than Hitler, after all.

"Besides, he's a lawyer," Samuel quipped. "Much scarier."

"Not as scary as I'm gonna be if these layabouts don't *do some chores!*" Amos bellowed with jocular false aggravation. "Heidi, go get the other goblins. Aliza, come help me so I don't burn the kitchen down."

"'Kay, Dad!" Heidi said, skipping upstairs to retrieve the younger Aumans.

"Liza, when you're done…" Sam reached into his bag, yanked out the latest issue of *Detective Comics*, and tossed it at the girl with a wink. "This issue is good, you know, for *Batman*."

"Thaaaanks!" giggled Aliza, sticking her tongue out at her Superman-loving uncle. "Compare 'em after dinner?"

"I'll win."

"Liiiiza!"

"Coming, Dad!"

Aliza threw her backpack beside Heidi's and tucked the comic under her arm, glancing down at the Contract on her chest as she did so. Her family had nearly made her new acquisition slip her mind, but seeing it, *feeling* it, reminded her that she needed to try and use it at some point. Maybe after dinner, when she had relative privacy in her room?

"Ah! I see you actually read your history book!"

Amos' voice was quiet, but cheerful. When Aliza looked up, she was utterly shocked to see a sun-colored triangle stuck above his heart. It seemed that she wasn't the only Master in the Auman household.

"You've got one too," Aliza said. Amos leaned against the kitchen counter and smiled widely.

"I was beginning to worry you'd never actually study!" he chuckled. "Being fair, I only put it in your book last night, so I guess you noticed it quicker than I thought you would."

"Heeey, I study sometimes!" Aliza whined with a smirk. Amos scurried over and shut the kitchen door to give him and his daughter some privacy, no doubt not wanting either Sam or his other daughters to hear their conversation and have them both committed.

"So, are you the Master that Satan mentioned, the one that gave up the Contract?" Aliza queried, tapping the Contract to Zone N-1 with the rolled-up comic in her hands. She could have sworn that she saw Amos wince, but he turned towards her with a bright smile.

"Ah, no. I just happened across it," Amos said with a shrug.

"And you didn't take it?" Aliza said. "It's *Hitler's* Contract..."

"Yes," Amos sighed, his eyes briefly flitting to the Contract and blazing in a way that Aliza hadn't seen before. Amos almost never got angry with his children, so seeing true fury in those turquoise eyes was startling. Quickly, however, his pupils flitted back to his daughter's face and familiar affection returned to his irises.

"Frankly, I thought about it, but you come first," Amos said. "And I know you've been angry lately...well, angry for a while, and reasonably so. You have more reason to have a personal vendetta against Heydrich than I do after what you went through in his camp. I know that's why you always play around with that dagger you took from him."

"You know about that?!" Aliza yelped, earning a chuckle from her father as he reached out and ruffled her short hair.

"Demon girl, I know *everything*," he teased. Aliza snorted, pushing his arm away with the rolled-up comic.

"How long have you been a Master?" she asked, and Amos blew out a long, contemplative breath and counted off his fingers.

"Siiiince...45. A little bit before I was reunited with you and Heidi, actually. I started out with just one Zone, but..." He pulled off one triangle and revealed a second one underneath. "I managed to earn a few more. Impressed Ha-Satan."

"*You* impressed him?" Aliza blurted in disbelief. "You, uh, don't seem like the type."

"What, you think I'm too *nice* to be a Master?" chuckled Amos.

"Well...yeah."

"I appreciate that, sweetie, but I'm *nice*, not *stupid*," Amos said. "I think there were...a few good men even in the SS, but almost all the rest were irredeemable. And I *do* think that monsters should get what they put into the world. Not to...talk about bad things too much, but my first Contract was for someone who put me through a lot."

Anger again flashed in Amos' eyes as he brushed his thumb against his Contract. "I was more than happy to give him what he deserved, and I'm happy to keep at it. And as for you!"

Amos patted his daughter's shoulder. "You're a tough gal, and hopefully now that you can give those monsters the real what-for, you can stop brooding in the mornings and start getting to school on-time."

"No promises," Aliza joked before beaming at her father. "Thanks, Dad, for thinking of me."

"Not a problem, sweetie. And hey! Now you and me can hang out together in Hell! "

"We can?" Aliza giggled.

"Haven't been down yet?"

Aliza shook her head.

"I have a feeling you're not gonna read the Manual since it's not a comic," Amos sighed, gesturing to the comic book in the girl's hands. "That's fine: nobody ever reads it. I can show you a lot of the ropes. When you go down, you'll see a mirror. Just draw N-7 in the mist. I know it sounds odd, but you'll see what I mean."

"That's not the oddest thing I've heard today," Aliza said, and Amos chuckled.

"You'll get used to it! Later! No punishing Hitler until after dinner."

"Yes, sir!" Aliza said, giving him a salute.

"Put that book down and grab some plates! Let's *actually* set the table."

Aliza obeyed, and they all enjoyed a typical Auman family dinner. Shaina whined and cried for a little while about having to do the dishes, but finally stopped blubbering when Samuel distracted her by asking her to perform a headstand. Shaina did so, and forgave her sisters for their sin when they gave her a raucous round of applause.

Uta kept refusing to eat any chicken because "ladybugs only eat aphids" and only nibbled at her food when Amos convinced her that ladybugs, being carnivores, would surely eat a little bit of meat if they were big like her.

Samuel and Amos talked about their respective love lives—Samuel was diligently writing Hana, Amos was planning on a second date with his co-worker Devorah. Shaina demanded that her father hurry up and marry her so they could have a mama, and Amos blushingly declared that love was a long process.

Aliza chimed in a few times during the dinner. She complimented Heidi when she pulled out her sketchbook and showed off a design for a dress she was planning on making. She argued with Uncle Sam about comic books. While she loved spending time with her family, however, Aliza could still feel the *thrum, thrum* of the Contract on her breast, reminding her of her new power. Eventually, she could bear the excitement no more and quickly shoveled the last of her dinner into her mouth.

"Plate's clean!" she declared, nearly choking on her

chicken as she did so. "May I be dismissed? I'm really tired!"

"All that chore-dodging got ya tuckered out?" Amos teased with a wink. "You're dismissed. Have a good rest, hun."

"Feelin' okay, sis?" Heidi asked, no doubt wondering why her sister, who typically stayed up until 1 AM, was turning in so early.

"Are ya turnin' semi-nocturnal like a rabbit?" Utas squeaked, and Aliza chuckled, twinging the little antenna on Uta's ladybug headband.

"I'm fine! Long day, tired, gonna get some extra sleep."

"Have a good night," Sam said, and Aliza paused to give her uncle a hug before scurrying up to her and Heidi's shared room. She bolted behind her black curtain, and just before she fell onto her bed, she reached into her drawer and yanked out the shimmering SS dagger.

"All right, you bastard..." she whispered, laying down on her stomach with the knife in her hands. "Let's see if this works."

Squeezing her eyes shut, she did as Ha-Satan had instructed and thought: *I want to go to Zone N-1.*

There was a rushing sensation not dissimilar to what she had felt when Amos had taken her and her sisters to a somewhat shoddy carnival and let them ride on a rickety rollercoaster. This exhilarating feeling, however, was matched by an unnatural frostiness, as though Aliza was going down a ski slope in the middle of a blizzard.

Then, quite suddenly, the cold was gone, replaced by a sensation of coziness. At first, Aliza thought that she was still in her bed, but when she lifted up her head, she realized that she was lying down on a giant silver throne.

"Huh..." Aliza mumbled, sitting up and tightly

grasping Heydrich's dagger, which she had managed to bring with her into the very depths of Hell.

Hitler was nowhere to be seen, nor Heydrich, nor any of the other Nazi assholes promised on her Contract. Aliza was sitting in a strange hexagonal room, on a silver throne. Humming curiously, she hopped off her seat and let her gaze sweep the area.

Her eyes landed upon the floor: there was a giant glowing upside-down yellow triangle on the ground which was the black room's only source of light.

"Cool…" Aliza muttered before letting her eyes wander. First, she turned to look at the silver throne that she had landed on. There were crimson letters on the onyx wall right above the glistening plush seat.

Here Sits
The
God of
~~Zone N-1~~
Nazi-Land

Somebody had obviously edited the sign, clumsily crossing out the bottom Zone number and replacing it with their own scarlet scrawl, but Aliza liked it. *The God of Nazi-Land*, that was her now.

And she was apparently not the first either. Aliza glanced at the wall beside the throne and found it to be occupied by several portraits. Above those portraits was a golden plaque, edited just like the letters above the throne: **The Masters of ~~Zone N-1~~ *Nazi-Land*.**

It almost reminded her of the school portraits that hung on the walls of their synagogue's Hebrew classroom: six severe pictures were carefully arranged beneath the plaque. One was her own, which made Aliza raise an eyebrow because she certainly didn't remember taking such a picture. Beneath her portrait was a small plaque: "Master 6."

"So who was number five?" she muttered, but the wall offered no answers. There was a plaque which read "Master 5" right before Aliza's portrait, but it seemed that the former Master had gone out of their way to erase all traces of their Masterhood from the Zone: the glass was smashed, and their picture had been taken out of its frame.

"Weird…" Aliza muttered, turning to the next corner of the room: there was a large, misty mirror with a silver frame and a golden eye perched atop.

"Oh," Aliza muttered, curiously walking towards the glass. *This is the mirror thing Dad mentioned, the way to let him into my Zone.*

She rubbed her hand along the glass, banishing the mist for a moment and revealing that the surface of the mirror only offered a view of swirling shadows. Humming, she tried to remember her father's instructions on how to let him in but couldn't.

Didn't he say something about a manual…? Aliza thought, turning around to face the other wall. There were two clocks there, one which was labelled "Earth" and one labeled "Zone." For her to keep track of her time? She shrugged and let her eyes wander to the Master Room's final feature: a podium with a book resting on it.

"There we go," she muttered, trudging towards it. The Manual was thicker than all of her textbooks put together. *Will to Power: A Manual for Masters. Vol. 78206.* Wrinkling her nose, Aliza decided that she should at least skim it to see if it would tell her how to operate the mirror. She started with the first chapter.

Masterhood: Congratulations! Whether you were assigned your Contract by the Board of Punishment and Purification or were given it by another Master, you have become a member of a highly privi-

leged class. As a Master, you will be blessed with many advantages that go well beyond Godhood within your Zone.

First, as a Master, your duties may call you to Zones which are set to violent, dangerous, or utterly barbaric time periods. You might be concerned about your health: can you catch a rare, extinct disease in the Zone? If, somehow, you are injured in the Zone, will this injury be fatal? What about food, water, and hygiene if you spend most of your time in the Zone? Will your body be all right?

Please don't worry about these trifles! Ha-Satan and the Board of Punishment and Purification have seen to it that you will be safe and well cared for within your Zone. Any food which you eat within the Zone will nourish your body on Earth. Likewise, so long as you keep yourself clean and healthy within the Zone, it shall be so on Earth. Caring for yourself will be easier as a Master than it ever was as a normal human!

Concerning injury: if you are injured within your Zone, please immediately leave. No injury which you sustain should follow you. Once you exit the Zone, you may return immediately. Leaving the Zone and returning will render you completely healed upon your return to the Zone. Please note: this will not apply to injuries sustained on Earth.

*Should you be fatally injured by another Master within then Zone, for example during a **Master Battle,** you will lose your Master status and your opponent will claim all of your Contracts, but your soul will be returned safely to Earth. A human who is killed within the Zone is permanently barred from future Masterhood.*

"Master Battle?" Aliza repeated, and fortunately, she turned a few pages and found a new chapter.

Master Battles: A Brief Overview.

As the Master, you have unlimited power within your Zone. You may, however, find collaboration with other Masters to be useful in pursuing justice against the sinful: other Masters may possess Subjects which could be useful should you wish to utilize them against your own Subjects. Former lovers, friends, and close companions may be placed in different Zones, after all.

However, you may also decide that you desire to be the Master of a Zone which is already owned by another. Perhaps, for example, you feel that another Master is **not adequately punishing their Subjects.** *In such a case, it may be optimal for you and your rival to agree to a Master Battle.*

Simply put, a Master Battle is a battle to the death between two Masters. The victor of this fight will gain all of the Contracts owned by the other. This will not apply if a Master kills another Master on Earth: the battle must take place in a Zone in order for a Contract to be transferred.

Please note: a Master will have significantly more power and energy in their own Zone compared to what they will possess should they choose to enter another Master's Zone. For this reason, it is highly recommended that you only engage in a Master Battle in your own Zone or a neutral Zone hosted by a third party. To enter another Zone for purposes of a Master Battle, simply use the Looking Glass.

"'Kay, but how…?" Aliza muttered, becoming frustrated as she flipped through the Manual. This was beginning to feel less and less like being given the power of a God and more like some sort of homework assignment.

The Manual was dense, and poorly indexed, and so Aliza didn't manage to find the section which explained the Looking Glass. She did, however, find herself stopping when she found a chapter that was entirely written in blood red-text.

Command*: As Master, you have been given the power of complete control over the soul of the Subject you have been awarded. While this means that you have the power to do anything you wish* **to** *them, you also have the ability to force your Subject to do whatever you want.*

This power, known as the **Command***, allows you to override the free will of your Subject. A Command requires ironclad will and intent, and must either be spoken or written down. To use a Command, solidify your will, and then say or write down what you* *want your Subject to do. A Command will be ineffective if the Master does not truly wish to use it.*

Warning: once you use this power, there is no going back.

"Command, huh?" Aliza muttered, shutting the book and sighing. She would have to wait until tomorrow to invite her father into her Zone. For now, the dagger in her hand felt weighty, and the knowledge of the power she possessed was eating away at her. She wanted to use it. She *needed* to use it.

Aliza turned away from the Manual. There was a hallway which led to a smooth black door marked with yet another yellow triangle. Tightening her grip on Heydrich's blade, she marched out the door, ready and raring to use her power.

▽

Chapter
THREE

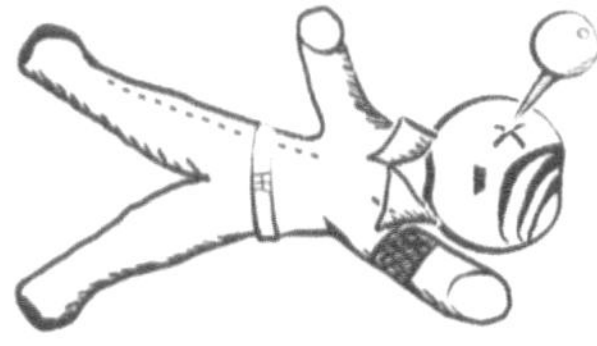

Aliza emerged into a space that was somewhat familiar: a place she had seen when watching old propaganda movies that had ended with Hitler being splattered by a mallet and sent down to the Devil. It was an office that was more wide than grand: she could imagine that the long walk a visitor would have needed to take in order to get from the door to the desk would have been daunting since there was nothing but blank space between each end of the room. Blank space and sunlight spilling in through the plethora of windows that offered a view of Nazi Berlin.

This was Hitler's office, then. His Reich Chancellery, or at least an imitation of the one that had been utterly decimated during the war, the one that Hitler had used, sat in, murdered from.

Aliza perked up her ears and realized that there were voices coming from behind the double doors through which an unfortunate guest of the Führer would have entered to visit the ruler of the twelve-year Reich. Since she didn't see her Subjects here, that must have meant they were in the other room.

Aliza, brazen and eager to use her Contract, almost ran right in before she stopped and remembered that just because she was a God didn't mean she was bulletproof. The Manual had said that she could get injured or even die in the Zone, and even if Zone-induced injury or death wasn't permanent, she didn't want to lose the Contract before she even got to use it.

"Okay…uhm…I'm bulletproof now," she whispered, and the Contract on her chest glowed with a golden light as she felt a wonderfully warm feeling of power flow through her. Satisfied that her wish had been fulfilled and her Subjects could not harm her, Aliza strutted though the door.

BAM!

Aliza's intuition was good, because almost immediately, somebody tried to blow her brains out. Before she could even think of giving a Command or using her magic, however, someone called out: "Heydrich, wait a minute!"

That was a familiar voice: a voice that Aliza had heard on the radio when she was little, a voice that had insisted she wasn't even human. Joseph Goebbels, the propagandist of the Third Reich.

The smoke cleared, and Aliza Auman's new Subjects were revealed.

There was Heydrich, the tall, blond, blue-eyed face of Nazism. Always front and center in her nightmares. This time, however, Heydrich wasn't snarling like the rabid dog he was. Instead, he wore an expression of exhausted disdain as he aimed his gun at the God of Nazi-Land and huffed in disappointment. The Hangman of Prague must have realized that the Master had been wise enough to render herself bulletproof, and as soon as he realized that...yes, there, fear started to shine in those frosty blue eyes.

"It's only a young girl...or is it a boy?" came a soft mumble, and Aliza's eyes flitted to a much shorter man with slightly messy light brown hair, grey-blue eyes concealed behind misty pince-nez glasses, and a chinless face that was covered in sweat. Heinrich Himmler, Reinhard Heydrich's chief, the *Reichsführer* of the SS, the ultimate mastermind of the death camps. He squeaked like a frightened hamster as he bowed deeply towards the Master.

"Ah! Delighted to meet you, new Master!" Himmler cried, cowardly liar that he was.

"You simply must forgive Heydrich," another voice said, and Aliza turned. A corpulent man with a charming little smile was sitting at a table, all but crushing the poor chair under his massive weight. He was bedecked in the most ridiculous getup: a white uniform with so many medals pinned to his breast that it must have added an extra three or four pounds to himself.

He looked like a parody of fascism, but Hermann Goering, as ridiculous as he appeared, was no joke. The head of the Luftwaffe, former chief of the Gestapo, Hitler's second-in-command, the man who had transmitted the order to begin the Holocaust. Aliza remembered listening to the radio during his trial at Nuremberg and fuming with rage while Goering was permitted to sit on the stand and lie in front of the entire world. It had been utterly unfair that someone who had denied dignity and justice to millions of Jews had been given such niceties.

"He's just a bit jumpy, Master." Aliza at last bothered to look at Joseph Goebbels, who was leaning against a large table in the middle of the room. The propagandist was the shortest of the Subjects, and the ugliest besides: he possessed a ghoulish face with hollow cheeks and a strangely large head. Goebbels took two steps sideways, revealing that he had a limp leg. Aliza had heard that the propagandist was lame, but even she hadn't thought that the Nazis would be so hypocritical as to make a dark-haired, dark-eyed disabled man the herald of their perfect Master Race. So much for that.

Goebbels shuffled almost protectively in front of the last figure, who was standing in the shadows as though he hoped to go unnoticed by the new God of Nazi-Land. There was something about Adolf Hitler that simply could not hide, could not be ignored even when he clearly wished to be overlooked.

Goering spoke: "We simply weren't expecting a new Master so soon, we have—"

And Aliza Commanded for the first time: "***Shut up, all of you! Hitler, Heydrich, Goering, Himmler, Goebbels, all of you shut your fucking mouths!***"

In unison, every Nazi's lips became sealed. Goebbels, who almost certainly hated to be silenced, let out a muffled sound of discontent. Heydrich exhaled though his nostrils like an angry bull. Hermann Goering's cheerful smile dissipated, and he trembled. Himmler let out a yelp of pain that was cut off as he was forced to silence himself.

Aliza was confused for a moment: she hadn't even gotten to the torture yet, but all of the Nazis were quaking and making small, pained hums as though even this small Command was agonizing.

She realized after a moment that the Command itself somehow caused pain. Perhaps that made sense: she was forcing the soul to do as she wished, twisting it and crushing it with her godlike power and *making it* relent. It *would* hurt.

That was good to know.

"Heydrich, drop that gun and put your hands at your sides," she Commanded, and Heydrich obeyed. Aliza looked close and…yes, that was certainly pain flashing in those cold blue eyes.

"Huh," Aliza said. "Looks like you don't like that, hm? Well, that's good, but we can do better. Let's see…what first?"

Aliza had been fantasizing about something like this, a seemingly impossible scenario, for some time, and so she didn't have to think for very long about what she wanted to happen to her ex-tormentors. First, she turned towards Joseph Goebbels, the man whose lies had driven her neighbors and friends to turn on her and her first family.

"You, Goebbels," Aliza said, pointing Heydrich's dagger at the propagandist. **"You can open your mouth, and bite off your own tongue."**

Goebbels did, his jaw unlocking just long enough for him to stick out his tongue and chomp down. There was a terrible *crunch* and a squishing sound as the organ that had killed millions fell onto the floor and Goebbels collapsed to his knees, gargling on blood.

Aliza didn't consider herself a sadist: she didn't seek out small animals to torture and kill just so she could see blood and gore. Still, she was undoubtedly not the sort of girl who was grossed out by such things. Quite the opposite, actually. Amos had more than once needed to chastise Samuel for letting Aliza gawk at some of his bloodier horror comics.

Even Aliza, however, was shocked by the horrible, bloody scene that she had caused for a moment. She stared at the severed tongue and winced, but the feeling of nausea was quickly overwhelmed by a rush like nothing else. A fiery sensation that Aliza rarely felt, the very opposite of the helpless weight that oppressed her whenever she was reminded of her own weakness. A feeling of not only power, but righteousness. She was the God of Nazi-Land, after all, and she was going to make these sinful little ants wish that she would *only* rip out their tongues.

"All right...***Goering***," she said, turning towards the corpulent Luftwaffe chief. Goering's blue eyes became rimmed with tears. Aliza pointed at him with the dagger.

"You killed yourself before the Allies could kill you. Didn't wanna give us all the satisfaction of seeing you hang, huh?" she prodded, and Goering let out a muffled noise. She waved her hand dismissively and her eyes flitted about the room, landing upon a lovely piano resting in the corner.

"You avoided it then, no avoiding it now," Aliza chirped, pointing to the musical instrument. "***Go to that piano, yank out its strings, and hang yourself with the wire.***"

The Luftwaffe Chief stood up and slowly trudged towards the instrument to fulfill her Command. Aliza turned to her next target. "Himmler," she declared with a smirk. "You like making kids suffocate, hm?"

Himmler let out a muffled noise that might have been anything: an agreement, a denial, a plea for mercy. It didn't matter. Aliza glanced thoughtfully down at the SS dagger and considered her options for a moment before looking up and smiling.

"That cyanide pill you took was too good for you, coward!" she declared. "***Hold your breath until you suffocate. No passing out for you.***"

Aliza didn't actually know how long it would take for a person who couldn't pass out to kill themselves by holding their breath, but her Nazi guinea pig started to turn blue almost right away. He collapsed to his knees, one black-gloved hand grasping his chest, the other clawing at his neck as he kept making pathetic little muffled whimpers of pain.

"And you...." Aliza said, turning away from Himmler as the *Reichsführer* writhed about on the floor. She used the SS dagger to point right at the toothbrush moustache decorating Adolf Hitler's face. The late Führer was stiff as a board for only one moment before he let out a small, resigned sigh and stepped forward.

As the Führer emerged from the shadows, Aliza was a bit surprised. Hitler was average height, his hair was not black but dark brown, and his eyes...she wasn't sure why, but she had always thought that his eyes had been dark. It was hard to tell from black and white pictures, which were all she had ever seen of the man who had ruined her life, Amos' life, her sisters' lives, the lives of every man, woman, and child in Beth-Hadasha.

She had thought that his eyes would be dark and pitiless, black as a void, or maybe tinged with scarlet like the demon that he was. But Hitler's eyes were not only bright blue, the sort that Nazi scientists would have idealized, but a particularly striking shade of blue. A familiar shade of blue as well: his eyes were the same shade as those of her Uncle Samuel.

The thought that Hitler shared a physical feature with someone she loved so thoroughly made Aliza feel a wave of nausea that morphed into anger. He really had the gall to pretend to be human.

"Kneel down," she Commanded. Hitler winced. Aliza had seen Hitler a lot in her life: Hitler angry, Hitler stern, Hitler weary in the pictures and reels circulated of his last excursion out of the Bunker before his death in Berlin, but never Hitler in pain. It was quite an odd sight, initially so odd that she couldn't even take pleasure in it because it was unnatural in the same way that watching Slowpoke eat a mouse would be unnatural.

Of course, Aliza only had to think of all the times her sister had heard a dog bark and whimpered, of all the times her father had been touched too suddenly by a friend at synagogue and winced, for her resolve to harden into iron. Aliza briefly considered Commanding him to lick her shoe, but that would be gross for her as much as him. She settled on something simple: "***Bash your head against the ground. Hard.***"

Hitler did, ramming his forehead onto the hardwood floor and grunting in pain as he no doubt fractured his own skull. Blood started pooling under his head, staining his brown-not-black mop of hair.

"***Again,***" Aliza Commanded.

BANG! More blood, another muffled yelp.

"***Again!***" Aliza cried, breathless as a laugh tore from her body. Bloody as this was, it also somewhat reminded her of the old cartoons where Donald Duck or Buggs Bunny would smack Hitler in the face with a mallet. She realized, however, that if she kept at this, then the Führer would knock himself out, and that would be too good for him.

Aliza chewed on her thumbnail for a moment, trying to decide which torment to give the Führer first. Once, she had fantasized about watching Soviet soldiers break every bone in Hitler's body, a fantasy that had been ruined when Hitler had shot himself like a coward. A smirk stretched across the Master's face as she realized that she could now make him hurt himself much, much more.

"***Hitler, break every bone in your body, starting with the fingers on your left hand, then your left toes, then your foot, and keep going until you can't break any more bones.***"

In one fluid motion, Hitler reached up, grabbed his pinky, and pulled it back. *Crack!* Aliza had never actually broken a bone herself, but she remembered hearing Nazis break prisoners' bones at the Fox Farm. The wet sound and the scream that Hitler was unable to truly let loose made Aliza uncomfortable for only the briefest moment as it summoned memories of the Fox Farm before those memories became kindling for the vengeful fire in her chest. He was getting what he had given. An eye for an eye.

Speaking of which, last but certainly not least, she turned away from the Führer and towards Heydrich. Hitler was Hitler, and Hitler was the worst, but Heydrich had been the one to shut her in the Fox Farm and kill her first father. It was his face that had haunted Aliza's nightmares for as long as she could remember. She had been dreaming of making that face contort in pain, and now it only took a few words.

"***Kneel down, asshole***," Aliza declared, and Heydrich did, his icy mask briefly fracturing as the Command brought about a wave of agony. Smirking, Aliza held up the dagger.

"Recognize this?" she queried, and Heydrich's fury-filled eyes flitted to the blade, widening in surprise as recognition filled his lake blue irises. Aliza had heard many times that when Heydrich had been alive, his memory had been impeccable. She wondered if he recognized her as much as the blade now.

"Yeah," she sneered. "Ya dropped this at the Fox Farm. You were keeping me there, me and my sister."

Heydrich exhaled sharply out of his nostrils, making a sound in the back of his throat that was either a grunt of pain or a curse that he couldn't speak.

"Ah, don't worry. You can have it back. Here..."

Aliza reached out, offering Heydrich his SS blade. She had once dreamed of being able to stab him herself, but now that she had this wonderful power, she had a better idea.

"You're the Man with the Iron Heart, right?" Aliza chirped. "That's what he called you."

She nudged her head towards Hitler, who was blinded by tears as he slammed his own wrist against the ground, shattering it.

"Let's see how true that is!" Aliza said. "***Take this blade and carve out your own heart.***"

Heydrich grabbed his dagger, winced as though even holding it was somehow setting his soul aflame, and then turned the blade towards himself, plunging it into his chest. Aliza stepped back, letting her gaze linger on Heydrich for a moment before she realized that something was missing.

"You can all open your mouths to scream," she declared, and they did, their screams almost deafening her at first before anger and horrible memories morphed the Nazis' howls into pure music.

Aliza remained down in Hell for some time, making the Nazis break themselves over and over. Every Command, every time she made Hitler slice off his own nose or Heydrich chop off another body part, made disgust venture a bit further away and made an intoxicating sensation of righteous power flow through her.

"Hey, demon girl, get up!"

And then, suddenly, she was in bed, and her father was shaking her out of the Zone with a smile on his face.

"Up, kiddo, c'mon, burning daylight!" Amos said, earning a long groan from Aliza. Being yanked out of a nice dream was already annoying, but being pulled away from watching Hitler beat himself up? She grunted irately at her father.

"Uuuuuup," Amos insisted, shaking her until she let out a shout of surrender and demanded that he get out so that she could change.

Her father chuckled and skittered out of her and

Heidi's room, and hardly had he left when Aliza looked down and realized with not a small amount of worry that Heydrich's dagger was no longer in her hand.

"What the...?" she muttered, searching her blankets and looking under her pillow. The dagger was nowhere to be found.

Shit! It stayed in the Zone! Aliza realized before calmness washed over her. She was the God of Nazi-Land, after all: it wasn't a big deal. Maybe Amos would know how to get it back, and if not, it was more useful to her in Hell than in her underwear drawer.

Quickly, Aliza changed. The faster she got to school, after all, the faster she could "fall asleep" at her desk and head back into the Zone. Maybe she could even take advantage of Miss Miller's suspicion that she had some sort of disease and spend the rest of the day lying down in the nurse's office.

Aliza donned her usual dark attire, this time putting on a pair of shorts that typically went under Miss Miller's dress-code radar, before dashing downstairs.

"Hey, you're up!" Heidi cried happily, and Aliza smiled at her sister. Frankly, even if it was annoying to get yanked out of the Zone, she would have wanted to leave early today anyway. If that strange man from yesterday was still stalking around Beth-Hadasha, she didn't want Heidi to walk to school by herself.

"I'm becoming a morning person," declared Aliza in her most exaggerated grouchy voice. "Dad, gimme some coffee."

"If that's what'll do it for you," Amos said, pouring her a small mug. "Sugar?"

"Lots. And milk!"

It was pretty nice, all things considered, to share an extra meal with her family. Uta had switched from ladybugs to rabbits and nibbled on an apple slice while scratching her bunny-ear headband. Shaina blabbered about her next gymnastics competition which she was certain she was going to win. Heidi begged their father for a slightly increased allowance so she could buy an adorable dress that she had seen in the shop yesterday. Aliza chatted with her sisters a bit before leaning close to her father.

"Hey, uh, sorry I forgot to let you in last night," she whispered. "I kinda forgot what you said about how to make the mirror work. And that Manual's too big."

"Ha! No problem! I didn't wanna intrude. When you're down later tonight, just remember: draw 'Zone N-7' in the mist on the mirror."

"N-7 on mist mirror. Got it, I think!" Aliza declared.

"Atta girl," Amos chuckled, sipping from his coffee. "I admittedly haven't read much of the Manual myself, but I'm sure we can pool our knowledge together."

"Uh huh. Hey, uhm, speaking of Zone knowledge, I brought Heydrich's dagger down with me and now it's gone."

"Ah! Should have warned you about that. The dagger's probably an Artifact."

"Arta-what?"

"Manual explains it better," Amos said with a shrug. "It's an item that's sort of...attached to a soul? I have one of my own..."

His voice trailed off gloomily and he bit his lip, shook his head, and plastered a smile back onto his face. "It's basically an item that holds such a strong emotional signif-icance to someone that the Contract mistakes it for part of a soul, so it gets dragged down. I think the issue is that the dagger isn't yours, it's Heydrich's, and once an Artifact goes into a Zone, only its owner can take it out. Sorry, sweetie, should have warned you."

"It's okay," Aliza assured him. "It's more useful down there."

"Just, you know, keep a tight leash on Heydrich when you head back down. Make sure he's not gonna try anything. Make sure he gives it back to you and just keep it in the Master Room. None of them can go in there without your permission."

"Got it! Thanks, Dad."

"What are you two whispering about?" Shaina squeaked.

"We're trying to decide who the ugliest person at this table is," Amos lied quickly. "We both think it's probably me, but we should put it up for a vote. Everyone who thinks Dad's the ugliest, raise your hand."

Everyone except Heidi raised their hand, which led to her being proclaimed the favorite daughter of the day. The Aumans finished off breakfast, Aliza quietly offered to invite Amos to her Zone when she returned after school, and with that, she and Heidi set off.

Heidi was happy to have her sister by her side, an assurance that she wouldn't be messed with this morning. Aliza, meanwhile, was on edge the whole trek to school. She didn't allow her guard to drop until they were past the gate and in the front yard. No sign of the strange man from yesterday. Maybe he really had just been a bumbling visitor looking for the bus stop. Good, then. Beth-Hadasha already had enough Nazi problems.

As Aliza scanned the schoolyard, however, she spotted Yonah Meckler chit-chatting with some of his friends. There was a sun-colored triangle stuck right above his heart. Yonah Meckler was a fellow Master.

Huh, thought Aliza as Yonah looked at her, saw the Contract to Zone N-1, and offered a small, knowing nod. She supposed it made sense. Someone like Yonah *would* be a merciless Master, though Aliza didn't know why he would bother picking on innocent Heidi if he had actual Nazis to torment.

Yonah started to approach the Auman sisters, hands tucked into his pant pockets, his posture casual bordering on submissive.

"Hey, uh..." the boy said, keeping a slight distance and glancing at Heidi. Aliza's sister clutched at her long blonde locks and started to scooch behind the God of Nazi-Land.

"Uh, Heidi, sorry about yesterday," Yonah said, raking a hand through his curly chin-length hair. "Was just, uh, y'know...anyway, I'm sorry."

He almost certainly wasn't really sorry: he simply wanted to make peace with Aliza now that she knew his secret. Aliza glanced at her sister, who bowed her head and muttered something incoherent.

"Uhm...Liza..." muttered the teenage boy, touching his bruised cheek and glancing down at the Contract on the girl's chest. "Can we...uh...?"

"Negotiate?" Aliza said, and that earned a chuckle from Yonah.

"I was gonna say *talk*," he mumbled. Aliza felt Heidi squeeze her arm. Normally, she would have told Yonah to go to Hell (she wondered how many times she had ironically told him that before), but curiosity made her decide to be diplomatic. It would probably be better if she could convince Yonah to focus his anger on the Nazis he owned rather than her sister. Heidi would benefit from some sort of peace treaty.

"Head to homeroom, sis," Aliza instructed, gently pulling her arm from her sister's grip. "I'm gonna see if we can compromise."

Heidi let out a small chuckle at that—Aliza's idea of *compromise* was usually to put whoever was opposing her in a headlock. Nevertheless, she obeyed, scurrying inside and leaving Aliza with her fellow Master.

"Uhhhh...ditch?" Yonah offered, gesturing towards the front gate. "Before Miller gets here."

Aliza would usually refuse, not out of any deference to her participation grade, but simply because there wasn't much to do around Beth-Hadasha if and when she *did* ditch. She would only ever ditch if Heidi did it with her, and A+ student Heidi Auman would *never* ditch.

Aliza also wasn't particularly fond of the notion that she might be spotted ditching *with* Yonah Meckler. People would get the wrong idea. The gossip-happy girls of Beth-Hadasha would be giggling about it for years.

Whatever, though. Aliza already didn't much care for other peoples' opinions and assumptions. Miller would probably be expecting her to call out sick anyway. Heidi might worry a little, but she would certainly be happy if Yonah Meckler agreed to leave her be from now on. And if Heidi didn't have to worry about bullies anymore, that potentially meant more sleep for Aliza, and more time in Nazi-Land.

"Where to?" Aliza asked.

"My place?"

Aliza scrunched up her nose.

"My mom will be there, but she'll be plastered," Yonah sighed. "Look, I was kinda hoping to ask for your help with something anyway, and you being a Master makes it better. What Zone?"

Shoving her hands into her pockets, Aliza rocked on her heels, building up some dramatic tension before proudly proclaiming, "Zone N-1."

"Hoooooly shit!" Yonah laughed. "You're the God of Nazi-Land! I was hoping to impress you with my Zone N-6."

"Ya don't impress me, Meckler," said Aliza, gesturing to the purple mark on his face. Yonah's single unbruised cheek once again flushed scarlet.

"Errr...whatever. Bygones and all that. You impress *me* either way. You're a tough bitch, and you're Hitler's Master. So...shall we?" He gestured to the open gate.

"All right," Aliza said. Really, she wasn't all that concerned about going to the house of a boy. She didn't actively *try* to repel boys with her looks, but she had never been offered a date, unlike pretty Heidi, who despite being bullied rather often was also the object of many a crush. Aliza didn't care about romance very much and was happy that most kids her age feared her in place of desiring her.

"I've gotta get back before the end of school, though," Aliza said, hastily following Yonah out of the schoolyard gate and keeping an eye out as they scurried towards the Meckler household. "There was a creepy guy chatting with my sister yesterday. Gotta walk her home."

"Gotcha."

Yonah's house was a short trek away from the school: a run-down little place so covered in weeds that Aliza couldn't even tell what color the building was. The gutters were rusted and filled with dead leaves. The glass on the windows was cracked and foggy, and the blinds on every one were drawn shut. If Aliza hadn't known that it was Yonah's home, she would have assumed that nobody had lived here for years.

"Ma, I'm home!" Yonah cried. "Gotta friend here!"

A horrid stench assaulted Aliza's senses as she followed Yonah into his house, an odor worse than Slowpoke's feces: some combination of booze and backed-up sewage that somewhat reminded her of the scent which had pervaded the barracks at the Fox Farm. The Mecklers' household was a mess of dirty clothes strewn about, empty bottles laying hither and thither, and...

"Chickens...?" muttered Aliza, glancing into the

kitchen and raising a brow when she saw three rusty cages housing clucking hens.

"Racoon broke into the outdoor henhouse," explained Yonah brusquely, wincing as movement came from the torn-up old couch. Yonah Meckler's mother emerged from a cocoon of crusty blankets, her dark hair a mess of curls and rats' nests. She regarded Aliza with bleary eyes and spoke in a slurred voice.

"She's the girl you talk 'bout?" Miss Meckler muttered, sounding both exhausted and disdainful. "She looks like a boy. You sure you're not a fag?"

"Ma, *please*..." hissed Yonah, gesturing desperately to the backdoor. "We're gonna be in the treehouse outside."

"Don't fuck," commanded Miss Meckler before returning to her coffin of blankets. Aliza would have rather returned to the Fox Farm than spend another minute in this house that was clearly toxic in more ways than one, and so she happily followed Yonah out into the backyard.

There was, indeed, a rather impressive treehouse back there, and when Aliza climbed up, she found that Yonah had turned it into a sanctuary, a home away from his awful home. Flash Gordon posters covered every wall, a sleeping mat was tidily laid out in one corner, and the roof had been decorated with stickers of stars and planets. There were books about astronomy piled up in one corner, and there was a small, cheap green typewriter sitting on the floor beside a satchel full of pages.

"Make yourself at home," Yonah said, shutting the thatch behind Aliza and regarding her with an embarrassed expression. "Sorry, uh, about that, my mom's...you know. Dealing with shit."

There were a plethora of ways to *deal with shit*, and it seemed that the Mecklers were wont to choose the worst coping mechanisms Aliza shrugged, however. Maybe she wasn't one to talk given how often she had battled Heydrich's ghost before she became his Master.

"It's fine. Uh, sorry about your mom," Aliza said. Sometimes, living in Beth-Hadasha with its populace of Holocaust survivors, it felt like "sorry about X" was just another way of saying hello.

"Being frank, I was kinda jealous of you and Heidi. Your dad seems nice. Real crapshoot, if you get a parent who deals with shit by giving out lollipops and hugs, or...well, Ma. Love her, but...yeah. Oh, you can look at that, if you want!"

Aliza had been cautiously peeking into the satchel of papers, and when she gave it a proper look, she discovered that it was about a hundred pages of a book-to-be. She wouldn't have believed that Yonah could write so much if his name weren't on the first page right under the title of the novel draft: *Zion Ten by Yonah Meckler*.

"Are you writing a novel?" Aliza asked. "*You?*"

"Yeah!" Yonah said, and Aliza had never seen the typically smug, posturing Yonah Meckler brighten up like Uta did whenever Amos asked for a fun fact about her favorite animal of the week. "It's a sci-fi book! I basically only go to school because Mr. Schwartz is great and his lessons really come in handy, plus I gotta double check shit at the library. It's about this alien race, and they come to Earth after they have a civil war because the last member of their royal bloodline is here, but they come during the war, and it turns out Hitler's already killed the monarch, so they end up bombing Berlin and..."

Off he went, enthusiastically describing the plot of his yet-unfinished novel, blabbering happily about the main-character's journey to save Earth and become an alien queen (Aliza was rather surprised that Yonah had made his main character a woman, and a warrior woman at that.)

Aliza listened intently, just as she did when her sisters jabbered about their hobbies. The book sounded decent enough, though Aliza likely would never read it even if it was published (the only books she read besides those required by school were the comic variety.) Either way, though, it was nice to watch Yonah cheerfully share something that clearly meant the world to him. Aliza liked this Yonah Meckler much more than the one she knew from school.

"...anyway, it's not done yet. I'm halfway through, I think."

"Lemme know when you finish. I'd read it," Aliza said, which earned a wide smile from her classmate. "Kinda surprised you managed to type this much. You hate English. You never do your homework."

"Homework sucks. I wanna write what I wanna write," Yonah said with a shrug. "I was gonna ask, though: you're more of a...boxing type than a creative type, and Ha-Satan usually picks artists and writers. At least for the top Zones."

"I draw sometimes," Aliza said, though doodles in her textbook probably didn't count towards rendering her as creative as Dante Alighieri. "And I've been thinking of ways to make Heydrich and Hitler cry for a long time. Don't need to be a writer for that."

"True," Yonah said, crossing his arms. "Anyway, for this job, I need a partner that's creative and isn't afraid to get their hands dirty."

"You picked the right gal, then," declared Aliza, carefully setting Yonah's manuscript back where it belonged and leaning against the wall of the treehouse, waving for him to speak. "What's this thing you needed help with?"

"This shit." Yonah reached under his sleeping mat and pulled out a familiar sheet of paper: it was one of the Black-Sun Brotherhood posters that Aliza had seen defacing the synagogue. Yonah had gone to the liberty of crossing out Hitler's face in a big red marker and had written some none-too-flattering things about the Führer in the margins.

"This march," Yonah said, tossing the marked-up poster onto the floor between them. "Bunch'a Nazi assholes coming in here and scaring everyone in town. But they have a legal right to it, to call us all liars and frauds."

"First Amendment," sighed Aliza, glancing sadly at the illustration of George Washington that shook hands with the crossed-out Hitler. She admittedly hadn't paid much attention during history class, but she was pretty confident that the first President would be gritting his false teeth if he saw that poster.

"Right. So the cops won't stop 'em, and nobody else in town wants to fight Nazis, so it's gonna be up to us. You and me, Zone Masters. and you having that..." Yonah gestured to Aliza's Contract. "Having *him*." He pointed to Hitler's defaced visage on the poster. "That'll make things easier."

"Uh...how?" Aliza asked. "I'm the God of Nazi-Land, sure, but I can't exactly yank Hitler's ghost outta the Zone and Command him to call all the neo-Nazis assholes to hurt their feelings. Uhm...I *can't*, can I?"

"Nope," chuckled Yonah. "Forgot you just got the Contract. I'm thinking more of a fight fire with fire sort of thing. Maybe Hitler or Himmler or Heydrich know something about this Nicholas Jackson guy. We gotta figure out a way to fuck up their little march without getting arrested. Let's meet here after school from now on, brainstorm, and yank any info we can outta your Subjects. Sound like a plan?"

Aliza pursed her lips into a tight line and nudged her head in the direction of the schoolhouse. "I wanna stop that parade too, but I'll only work with you on one condition: you and your friends don't touch my sister anymore. Deal?"

"Deal," said Yonah quickly before offering Aliza a smirk and saying. "But let me kick Heydrich in the balls at least once. I owe him for Terezin."

Aliza wasn't one to deny someone a justly earned strike of revenge. She reached forward, and the two young Masters sealed their truce with a handshake.

Chapter
FOUR

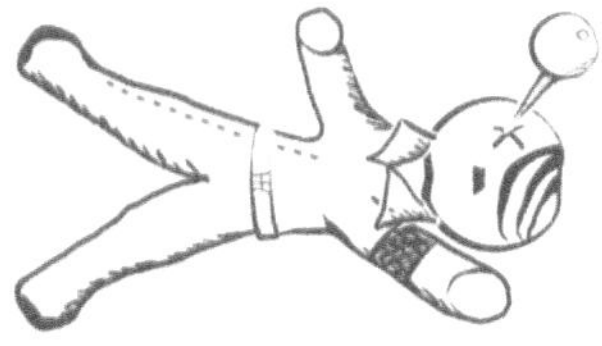

The next time she went down to Zone N-1, Aliza immediately hopped off the silver throne and walked over to the Looking Glass, pausing for a moment to stare at the golden eye carved on top before facing the misty surface.

"Oooookay," Aliza muttered, fighting to remember what Amos had told her before the recollection came to her. Using her finger and feeling like she was an eight-year-old drawing smiley-faces on the glass door of the shower, Aliza scrawled: *Zone N-7.*

The mist cleared, but the Looking Glass did not offer a reflection of Aliza Auman or the Master Room behind her. Instead, Aliza looked into the clear glass and saw her father sitting in a different Master Room. He was wearing a turquoise scarf, fiddling with the ends of it as he lounged on a silver throne that seemed slightly smaller than the one offered by Aliza's Zone. The crimson lettering above the throne boasted: **"Here Sits the God of Zone N-7."**

"Dad!" Aliza cried, and Amos grinned, jumped off the throne, and ran to the Looking Glass.

"Coming through!" he cried, and he stepped into Zone N-1 as though the mirror was nothing more than a doorway.

"If it isn't the God of Nazi-Land! What an honor!" cried Amos, bowing deeply towards his daughter, earning a giggle from the girl.

"Nice scarf, Dad!" she said. "Is that the Artifact you mentioned?"

"Yeah…gift from a friend," Amos sighed, straightening up and plucking at the end of the scarf. "I keep it down here. Stays safe that way, prevents Uta or Shaina from finding it and tearing it up."

Sadness was penetrating Amos' voice, and Aliza could only guess that her father's 'friend' had been one of the war's many casualties. She had no desire to pry, and so, in an effort to distract him, Aliza blurted the first thing that came to her mind: "Hey, uh, Dad, you didn't mention that Yonah Meckler was a Master."

The sorrowful cloudiness in Amos' turquoise eyes dissipated, and he smiled. "Oh! I sometimes forget myself! He never shows up at synagogue. Last time I saw him was last year's Purim party…and I was so drunk I could barely see my own hand in front of my face, much less a Contract!"

"At least you didn't end up like Uncle Sam."

"Haha! Arrogant Russians think they can handle anything. I'm shocked he still has a liver!"

"Religious mandate: he has to drink until he's really drunk. But the amount it takes for him to get there also makes him vomit and pass out."

"Let's not mock your uncle when he isn't present to defend himself, shall we? More pertinently: you didn't invite Yonah into your Zone, did you?"

"Not yet." Aliza said, and Amos let out a small sigh of relief.

"Ah! Good! Because lesson number one: don't ever do that," Amos declared, holding up one finger and shaking his head. Aliza raised a curious eyebrow.

"Why not?" she inquired, pointing towards the Master Manual that rested on its platform. "I read the Manual a little last night, it said that Masters can visit each other for collaboration…"

"And I don't suppose you read what *else* Masters can do to each other," Amos prodded with moderate anxiousness, tightening his grip on the end of his scarf.

"Kill each other," Aliza said, shoving her hands into her pockets. "To take each other's Contracts."

"Right-o. And you, demon girl, have the most desired Contract in all of Hell," Amos said, gesturing to the '*Nazi-Land*' painted above her throne. "Everyone wants to get at Hitler's soul. You should never invite anyone into your Zone."

"I invited *you* in."

"Well, first of all: I'm your dad, so I'm the exception. Second of all: you technically didn't. Not really. You see, any Master can walk into any Zone they wish. However, if they don't get an *official* invitation, they won't be able to bring any of their Subjects over, and they won't have any power in the other Zone. They'll be considered an Invader. On the other hand, if you trust someone and *do* wanna collaborate with them, you just face the Looking Glass, like so, and say…"

Amos stood before the Looking Glass, looking straight at the eye on top and declaring, "I hereby invite the current Master of Zone N-1 and their Subjects to enter my Zones."

The eye briefly flashed with golden light, and so did Amos' Contract. When the light faded, Amos turned to his daughter with a bright smile. "And there you go! Now, if you were to come into my Zone, you'd be considered a Guest. Whenever you like, you can come into my Zone and bring your Subjects."

Amos gestured to the door with the yellow triangle. "The key is to bring your Subjects along: your power is actually tied to your Subjects, so as long as they're in a Zone with you, you'll have at least some power. If you can't bring them, though, don't *ever* enter anyone else's Zone. And if you want Yonah to come over, don't give him a formal invitation or let him bring in any of his Subjects. He probably won't try anything—it would be suicide to attack you in your own Zone, the Master always has more power in their own Zone. Frankly, since I doubt Yonah read the Manual, he may not know any of this, but better safe than sorry. Don't want him to surprise you."

"Nope! Thanks, Dad! I'm glad *you* read the Manual."

"Haha!" Again, anxiousness invaded Amos' turquoise eyes and he began winding the end of his scarf around one finger. "Well…I didn't really read it all myself, but, uhm…anyway! You know about Guests, Artifacts, Master Battles…how about Commands?"

"Been using 'em!"

"All right!" Amos cried, clapping his hands together and nudging his head towards the Looking Glass. "Then I think you're good to go! I'm gonna head back to my Zone and leave you to your own devices."

"You sure you don't wanna come over and….?" Aliza drew her finger across her throat and then gestured towards the door to the Zone. "I mean, Hitler's here."

Briefly, Aliza could have sworn that she saw fire erupt in her father's turquoise eyes again, but then Amos grasped at his scarf and gave a strained smile, shaking his head. "I'm fine, hun. Think I wanna head back to Earth for a little bit. Have fun, stay safe, don't lose your Zone!"

"I won't!" Aliza declared, deciding not to push and

waving farewell as Amos stepped back through the Looking Glass. "Bye, Dad!"

Amos waved, and the glass became covered in mist again. Satisfied that she knew everything she needed to, Aliza marched back into the Zone and got back to her duties.

▽

Chapter
FIVE

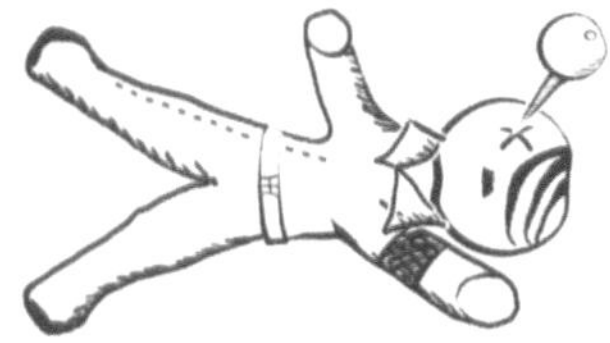

While Aliza had previously never possessed the inclination to ditch, now that she had the option of remaining in bed all day and tormenting Hitler, the prospect was tempting. She only ended up leaving her Zone, donning her pants, and going to school for two reasons: her father, who might have actually taken the Contract from her if she engaged in outright truancy because of it, and Yonah, whom she needed to talk to so they could arrange their first meeting.

Aliza expected Miss Miller to be absolutely ruthless: she had missed a day of school, after all, and during class she ended up ducking behind her textbook and Zoning out while her teacher blabbered on about the history of the Founding Fathers. Surprisingly, however, Miss Miller was relatively pleasant. She didn't force Aliza to pledge allegiance to the flag or nag her about wearing pants. She didn't yell at her for seemingly falling asleep in class but merely had Heidi shake her awake. When class was dismissed for lunch, Miller pulled Aliza aside while her classmates scurried to the cafeteria and asked after her health.

"You look a bit downcast, and I noticed you sleeping on your desk," Miller observed, dark eyes narrowing behind the pink glasses. "The nurse here at school can't do much, but if you need a doctor, I know one that's very good. A lady really should have a lady doctor, that's what I always say. It's impossible to discuss anything with a male doctor."

That actually fetched a chuckle from Aliza. She would have never thought she'd see Miss Miller so concerned for the wellbeing of her students given how often she tended to smack their knuckles raw. She almost felt like one of Miss Miller's pampered Maine Coons.

"I'm all right, ma'am," Aliza promised. "Just tired."

"Don't hesitate to say something if you're having another heart issue. My poor husband, God forgive him, he ignored his palpitations too long."

"I think I'm also just nervous about the march that's coming up," Aliza lied, waving her hand towards the windows. "It's all happening so suddenly."

"Ah. *That.*" Miss Miller huffed, glancing briefly at a poster on the wall which featured the Bill of Rights. "I don't think I'm allowed to say what I think about *that* during school hours, but as long as you stay inside, you'll be fine. They're just trying to provoke us into hitting them so they can sue us, you know. It's all about causing pain, one way or another. Win-win for them either way. The best thing to do is ignore them and pretend they don't affect you. They want a reaction, any reaction."

"Right..." sighed Aliza, fighting to keep a snarky, angry argument contained. *Ignoring them and pretending that they can't hurt us didn't go so well last time.*

"The First Amendment has to apply to everyone," Miss Miller noted. "Even Nazis."

"But…uh…not me when I don't say the pledge?" Aliza said, gesturing up towards the American flag, and she almost couldn't believe her eyes when that comment made a smirk come to Miss Miller's perpetually grouchy face.

"Cheeky, Miss Auman. I *do* seem to recall that you have detention to make up. But I'll let it slide given the circumstances. To lunch."

"Thanks, ma'am!"

Aliza went to the cafeteria and sat with Heidi, chatting about Uta's latest obsession (owls.) Yonah let the sisters be for a moment before he skittered over and thrust a note under Aliza's tray. Heidi winced, but Yonah didn't even seem to see her. He spared a wink at his fellow Master before running back to his friends.

"What'd he say?" asked Heidi as Aliza unfurled the note. She was surprised by how tidy Yonah's handwriting was, but she supposed that if he was an aspiring novelist, then he must have written before he'd ever had a typewriter. It must have been a long-forged passion.

Liza, invite me to your Zone! We can go right to the treehouse after school.

Yonah had drawn a little smiley face beneath that plea/proclamation. Aliza dug a pen out of her disorganized backpack, ignoring Heidi as she asked over and over what Yonah had said.

"Quit it, sis! None'a your business," Aliza huffed, elbowing her sister when Heidi tried to peek over her shoulder to read what Yonah had written.

Quickly, Aliza scrawled a response. *"Haha, no, not inviting you over, ass. I know what that does, nice try."* Then, with Heidi grumbling about how her sister had elbowed her too hard, Aliza bunched up the paper and tossed it right at Yonah's skull. The long-haired boy yelped, looked down, offered the smirking tomboy an amused smile, then reached down and carefully unfolded her response.

Yonah's smile disappeared, and he pouted like a toddler that had been denied the toy he'd asked for on Hannukah before he shrugged and gave her a thumbs-up.

"What was that all about?" Heidi asked.

"The truce," Aliza answered casually, violently tearing the top off of her chocolate milk carton. "I'm heading to Yonah's after school today. Tell Dad, will ya?"

"You're going to Yonah's?!" repeated Heidi, sounding as though she was choking on something even though she hadn't even taken a bite out of her sandwich yet. "Why?"

"Just to hang out," Aliza said, leaning back and loudly slurping her chocolate milk. Heidi gave her a look that perfectly mirrored Miss Miller at her most aggrieved.

"'*Hang out*," she repeated, and Aliza shrugged.

"We've gotta truce."

"I'm not sure I like this truce," grumbled Heidi, grabbing her fork and casting a vicious scowl at Yonah as he and some of his brainless friends started laughing about something.

"Hey, it's good for you," Aliza noted. "He hasn't bothered ya."

"It's been a day and a half," Heidi grunted, stabbing the fork in Yonah's direction as though she would have liked nothing more than to chuck the utensil at his head.

"It'll be longer if the truce becomes a peace treaty," Aliza noted.

"I just want him to leave me alone and jump off a cliff," Heidi huffed. "I don't wanna peace treaty."

"Well, he has a treehouse, so if ya want, I can see about pushing him out the window when his back is turned."

"Liza, I was...well, *mostly* joking," Heidi chuckled before heaving a sigh and yanking out her compact mirror, glancing at her flawlessly made-up face. "I just...never mind. Just don't be too long, okay?"

"Nope."

Despite Heidi's evident acquiescence to Aliza's after-school plans, the blonde girl gave Yonah a scowl worthy of an SS officer's daughter when she saw him in the schoolyard after the bell had rung.

"Hey, project?" Yonah said, ignoring Heidi and smiling at the God of Nazi-Land. Aliza nodded. She bade farewell to her sister and followed Yonah, ignoring the fact that she could just *feel* Heidi glaring at her back as she and the boy slipped out of the front gate together.

Aliza held her nose as they arrived at Yonah's home and passed through the Meckler household. Yonah paused only long enough to give his poor kitchen chickens some more food before he led Aliza out to the backyard and up into the treehouse.

"Zone out?" the boy said, sitting against the wall and offering Aliza his sleeping mat.

"You first," she demanded, plopping down on his sleeping mat, which was thankfully quite clean, in fact surprisingly clean given the state of his home. "You know what Zone I'm in."

"Hey, I was promised that I could have a go at Heydrich," Yonah noted with a childish pout. Yonah wasn't precisely a handsome boy, but when he did that, his features looked a lot less harsh. He almost seemed cute. "How am I supposed to do that if you won't let me become a Guest? I won't have any powers if I just walk in."

"I can just paralyze 'em," Aliza said. "You don't need magic powers to kick someone in the balls."

"Ha! True!"

"You go down first," Aliza insisted, waving for him to hurry up.

"All right, whatever." Yonah offered a casual shrug and leaned against the wall beneath his Flash Gordon poster, shutting his eyes. Aliza waited and waited, and when she was certain that the boy wasn't faking anything, she lay down and dove down into Zone N-1.

Yonah was already there when she landed in her Zone. The boy stood in front of the silver throne and stared up at the crimson proclamation right above it. "Nazi-Land?" he muttered. "I was wondering why Ha-Satan kept calling it that."

"I didn't do that," Aliza muttered, hopping off the throne, and Yonah shook his head.

"I know you didn't," the boy said. "When I asked Ha-Satan years ago if I could have Hitler's soul, he just said, 'Nazi-Land already has a Master.'"

"Hm…" Aliza glanced at the smashed portrait beside hers on the Wall of Masters, once more wondering about her mysterious predecessor. "Guess that's what they called it."

"C'mon. If I'm not gonna have any power while I'm here, I'm depending on you to make sure the Nazis are reined in," Yonah said, gesturing towards the door.

"Oh, they're reined in," Aliza promised, and indeed, as soon as they stepped out of the Master Room, the teens found themselves in the midst of the living room of the Berghof, where the exhausted Nazis were sitting in a semi-circle, whispering amongst themselves. Aliza had hardly crossed the threshold when a Command left her lips: "***On your feet, all of you. Hands at your sides, no moving.***"

The Subjects all obeyed, snapping to attention like good little soldiers, trembling with pain. Himmler was already starting to sob. Goebbels was cursing under his breath. Hitler was gritting his teeth and hissing. Aliza savored their agony for a moment before glancing at Yonah.

"Ah, you use Commands," the boy noted, tilting his

head sideways and gazing at the stationary Nazis with something resembling disappointment. He either didn't like to see them Commanded or, more likely, was disappointed seeing them up-close. It was, all things considered, a bit upsetting that so many lives had been torn to shreds by such pathetic excuses for men.

"Yep. That a problem?" Aliza grunted, and that fetched a chuckle from Yonah.

"Nah ah," the teen said, cracking his knuckles and strutting close to Heydrich. Smirking, he glanced at Aliza, who waved for him to go ahead. Yonah delivered a sharp kick to the Hangman's crotch that made Heydrich yelp in pain. Aliza's Command, however, kept Heydrich from sinking to his knees: he could only straighten back up and keep standing at attention, glaring daggers at the boy through tears in his eyes.

"I prefer more direct methods," Yonah declared, stepping back and cackling.

"Commands hurt 'em," Aliza noted. "Plus, it's extra fun to make 'em do shit to themselves. ***Hitler! Slap yourself in the face!***"

And Hitler obeyed, striking himself on the cheek so hard that he split his own lip and splattered his infamous face with blood. The dictator let out a howl of pain that made both teenagers laugh.

"See?" Aliza chuckled as Hitler's bloodstained face turned scarlet. "Adds insult to injury."

"Hey, hey, make Goering call himself a fat piece of shit, and then make him gouge his own eyes out!" Yonah begged, gesturing to the obese Luftwaffe chief.

"M-Master, that certainly isn't necessary! You know, I never had anything against your people! I actually allowed my wife and brother to help plenty of Jews, and I myself once helped this lovely Jewish couple—!" Goering started blubbering, but Aliza cut him off with a cold Command. ***"Shut your fat mouth and don't speak until you're spoken to."***

Goering did as he was told, slamming his mouth shut and whimpering, but Aliza didn't Command him again. Instead, she offered Yonah a smile. "I like the way you think, Meckler, but let's focus. Interrogation time."

The interrogation that commenced, however, was utterly fruitless. None of the Subjects of Zone N-1 had ever heard of Nicholas Jackson or the Black-Sun Brotherhood, and when Aliza Commanded them to offer suggestions for how to stop the march, the Nazis weren't helpful at all.

"You won the war," Hitler grunted with a genuinely curious glint in his eyes, his voice slightly slurred as his face swelled up from the self-inflicted slap. "Why are you allowing National Socialists to exist, much less march through your town?"

Anger consumed Aliza's chest as she was reminded of her powerlessness on Earth. The God of Nazi-Land offered the Führer a scowl. ***"On your knees,"*** she Commanded, and Hitler collapsed onto the floor with a whimper of pain that made Yonah snicker.

"You're fucking stupid, you know," Aliza said. ***"Say you're fucking stupid."***

"I'm fucking stupid," Hitler hissed, his bruised, bloody face flushing with humiliation.

"Say, 'I'm so stupid that I really believe the Jews rule the world.'"

"I'm so stupid that I really believe the Jews rule the world." Hitler's bright blue eyes were pouring tears, which almost gave Aliza pause because his eyes were so similar to those of her uncle, and she would have despised seeing Samuel cry. Nevertheless, she shoved that feeling aside and Commanded again.

"Keep calling yourself stupid and slap yourself in the face one hundred times."

Hitler of course obeyed, having no choice in the matter: scarlet-faced, he started smacking himself, punctuating every act of self-harm with a screech of, "Stupid! Stupid! Stupid!"

Yonah was nearly rolling on the carpet as he laughed and laughed. "That's great, Liza!" he cried before pointing to the rigid Hangman of Prague and demanding, "Do Heydrich next, c'mon!"

Happily, the God of Nazi-Land turned to the stationary Hangman. "Well, Heydrich?" she prodded. ***"Come on, how would you stop a march like this?"***

"Shoot them," came Heydrich's curt, forced response, and Yonah let out a loud guffaw upon hearing Heydrich's oddly high-pitched voice. Aliza realized right then that she had heard the Hangman scream quite a bit, but she hadn't actually heard him speak until this moment. She joined Yonah in derisively laughing at Heydrich, enjoying the sight of the furious embarrassment that burned in the proud Hangman's eyes.

"Oh, *that's* why the Black Foxes called him Billy-Goat Heydrich!" cackled Yonah. "Aliza, make him bleat like a goat, come on!"

"You heard him, Heydrich!" chirped Aliza, giddy at the thought of watching the man who had once shamed and dehumanized her degrade himself so thoroughly. ***"Drop the dagger, get on all fours, and bleat like a goat."***

"Fucking Jews!" snapped Heydrich, his high-pitched voice consumed with fury and humiliation as the Contract forced him to obey: he dropped the knife, fell on his hands and knees, and glowered viciously at the God of Nazi-Land with tears of pain and embarrassment pricking his ice blue eyes as he was forced to imitate a goat. Aliza and Yonah laughed and laughed, and Aliza had never felt so powerful, not even when she Commanded them to hurt themselves. Humiliation was its own form of punishment

The interrogation stopped after that. The teens spent the rest of the day punishing the Subjects, Yonah offering ideas while Aliza Commanded, forcing the Nazis to embarrass and hurt themselves over and over. By the time they were through, Yonah and Aliza still had no idea what to do about the Black-Sun Brotherhood, but the Nazis were all crying, and thus, the teenagers parted ways cheerfully.

"Same time tomorrow?" Yonah offered, and Aliza eagerly nodded. She could see why Ha-Satan had made collaboration between Masters possible: it was funner, somehow, to do it alongside a like-minded fellow.

"Tomorrow," she declared. "Definitely."

—————— ▽ ——————

Chapter

SIX

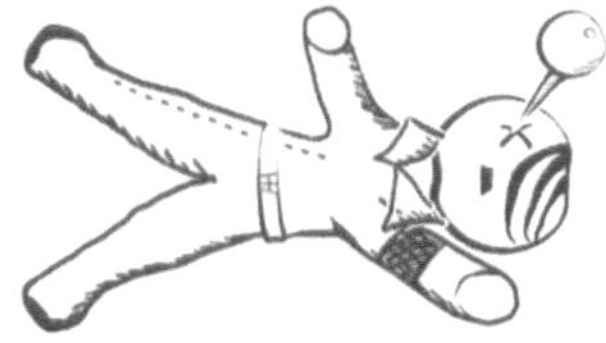

Amos hadn't given Aliza a middle name when he had adopted her, but if he had, then 'Procrastination' would have suited her perfectly. Aliza had always put things off until the last possible moment: homework, studying for tests, buying presents for Hannukah and birthdays.

In the weeks that followed her initial meeting with Yonah (who was just as much of a procrastinator as she), they both ended up putting everything off in order to torment the Subjects of Zone N-1. Admittedly, the teens didn't *intend* on wasting time: they kept interrogating the Nazis, hoping that one of them would have thought of a way to defeat their comrades.

But hearing Hitler scream and cry was rather distracting, and Aliza had to admit that Yonah was a rather creative fellow. The boy had confessed to skimming a few biographies about Aliza's Subjects in an attempt to learn more about them, to decipher how to leave them agonized and humiliated.

And so the duo continued on like this, retreating to

Yonah's treehouse every day and then whittling their hours away in Nazi-Land. Aliza found herself skipping dinners, Sabbath service, and playtime with her little sisters to spend time with Yonah. Her father didn't mind (in fact, every time Aliza announced that she was going to Yonah's house, Amos would respond with a chuckle and a delighted little smirk that made it clear he was already tallying up the price of the wedding.)

Heidi clearly *did* mind, though, as she would always regard such announcements with grumbles and glares. This made Aliza anxious at first because she didn't enjoy seeing her sister squirm, but it was ultimately for the greater good. If not to stop the Black-Sun Brotherhood then, at least, to make sure that the Nazis of Zone N-1 never got a break.

"...AND SO THAT, STUDENTS, IS WHY GEORGE WASHINGTON is the greatest President of all time," Miss Miller decreed as a conclusion to her lesson, gesturing proudly to the poster of the first President that she had hung on the chalkboard. "Not because he was the first, but because he was the first to step down. Given his popularity, Washington could have leveraged and hoarded the power of the presidency. Instead, he voluntarily relinquished it. The fragile nation which he left in his wake now stands as a mighty superpower because of this act of statesmanship."

Miller crossed her arms behind her back and paused for a moment, staring out at her students with an expression that was severe, but not grouchy, before she proclaimed, "The mark of a great leader, and for that matter a great human being, is to be offered power and refuse it."

Aliza bit her bottom lip and raised her hand.

"Yes, Miss Auman?" Miss Miller said, offering the ghost of a smile at seeing the typically disinterested Aliza actually participating for once.

"Maybe he was just tired?" Aliza suggested, and that fetched several chuckles from the students surrounding her. She expected Miss Miller to chastise her for that flippant remark, but instead the teacher simply hummed thoughtfully and glanced at the first President's portrait.

"If so, I can sympathize," she said. "Class dismissed!"

Quickly, the students started shoving their pencils and notebooks into their satchels, chatting cheerfully with one another.

"Sis, me and Dad have some serious digging work to do in the garden!" Heidi chirped after neatly packing up her textbooks. "There's gonna be a lotta dirt. Wanna help out?"

"Nope. Can't," Aliza said, struggling for a moment to shove her history textbook into her bag, which was utterly stuffed with candy bar wrappers and crumpled notes. "Heading to Yonah's place."

"*Again?!*" Heidi cried, her smile morphing into what could only be described as a look of aggravated horror. "You've gone to his place *every day* this week."

"We're working on a project," Aliza grunted, finally managing to shove her book into the satchel without making the entire thing combust.

"What project?" Heidi huffed, rising to her feet and casting a suspicious glance at Yonah. The boy was folding up some papers and carefully tucking them into his bag: he must have made notes during class, either more outlines and character graphs for his novel or more ideas for what to do to Hitler in Zone N-1. Aliza smirked and put a finger to her lips.

"Secret," she said, and that only made Heidi's scowl shift to her.

"...a secret project," Heidi said. "That *Yonah* can know but not me."

"Yep."

Heidi let out a yowl of frustration (which sounded so much like a cat getting its tail stepped on that Miss Miller turned with instinctual concern.) "Whatever!" the blonde girl snapped.

"See ya at dinner," Aliza said, chuckling with amusement at seeing her sister so red in the face.

"Maybe. If ya don't miss it again…" Heidi grumbled, but Aliza was already skittering out of the classroom door, smirking as Yonah loyally followed at her heels.

"Race?" he suggested, and Aliza wrinkled her nose.

"Not if I'm gonna lose."

"You *would* lose," Yonah bragged.

"And then you wouldn't be allowed to pick the punishments today."

Yonah snorted at the threat, and they skittered non-competitively out of the schoolyard and towards Yonah's treehouse. Once there, they dove into the Zone and spent an hour or so goofing off: Commanding Hitler to break his own bones, Commanding Goebbels to screech insults about himself until he was hoarse, Commanding Himmler to pull out his own teeth, Commanding Heydrich to carve insults into his own skin.

"He really hates that dagger," Yonah observed while the Hangman whined and winced as he was forced to shove his own blade into his flesh and scrawl, "*Asshole.*"

"It's an Artifact," Aliza noted, watching with satisfaction as Heydrich finished the last letter and then stood, bloody arms locked at his sides, glaring daggers at the two Jews through tears of pain, waiting for his next Command.

"An Artifact?" repeated Yonah curiously: evidently, Amos was correct, and the boy hadn't read the Manual.

While Heydrich stood by, Aliza recounted her tale of being held in the Fox Farm during its destruction, telling her partner how she had stolen Heydrich's dagger while he had been battling the Black Foxes.

"Cool!" Yonah exclaimed once she was through with her story. "I'd heard about the Fox Farm blowing up, but I didn't know that's where you were. The rumor in my neck of the woods was that the Bandit of Terezin stole his dagger."

"The what of what did what?" Aliza said.

"In Terezin Ghetto there was a person who used to sneak out and steal from Germans. SS men and their families and collaborators," Yonah explained, and while his voice bubbled with excitement, there was a note of sadness to it. He had never spoken of his experiences in Terezin, but from what Aliza had heard, the so-called "model" ghetto had been a nightmare that was no better than the Fox Farm.

"Then they'd leave little trinkets strewn around the Ghetto. Real hero," Yonah sighed. "I wouldn't be here if it weren't for them: they put a golden ring under our door, got us enough money for some black-market medicine when I was sick."

"Like a Jewish Robin Hood," Aliza observed, and Yonah nodded.

"Exactly!" he laughed "And there was a rumor that they stole something off'a Heydrich, but nobody could ever agree *what* they stole: dagger, ring, watch, it was *something*. Hey! Billy-goat!"

Yonah's gaze flitted to the Hangman of Prague, who was scowling down at the carving he'd been forced to make on his own arm. "What did the Bandit of Terezin steal off'a you?"

"*Be honest,*" Aliza Commanded for good measure,

and the Hangman winced in pain before speaking in a halting, furious tone.

"I don't know what you're talking about. That Jew never stole from me," he declared, and Yonah let out a huff of disappointment.

"Bah! Boring!" the teen boy cried, throwing his hands into the air before his eyes twinkled and he sat up. "Hey, while we're asking about rumors I heard in Terezin, asshole, did you actually put on the Czech crown?"

That made Aliza lift a brow in curiosity, and Heydrich, no longer under a Command, nevertheless answered bitterly: "It was a joke."

Yonah almost fell off his seat laughing. Aliza waited for him to catch his breath before she inquired, "What's this about the Czech crown?"

"There was a rumor during the war that when Heydrich here was made *Reichsprotektor*, the collaborators took him to see the old Czech crown," Yonah explained, pointing towards the scowling Hangman's messed-up blond hair. "The asshole was dumb enough to actually pick it up and put it on."

"Why's that dumb?" Aliza asked.

"The crown's cursed," Yonah declared confidently, and when that earned a derisive snort from Aliza, the teen boy regarded her with a crinkled brow.

"Really, Liza, *c'mon*," he said, gesturing about the Zone, chastising her for so readily dismissing the notion of a cursed crown when she owned a portion of Hell.

"'Kay, fair enough," Aliza relented, sparing a glance at her Subjects. Hitler had finished breaking every one of his fingers, Goering had gouged out both of his eyes, Himmler was almost out of teeth to pull, and Goebbels had run out of insults and so he collapsed, exhausted. The Subjects sat about, sobbing, quaking, waiting. They would need to receive more Commands in a moment, but Aliza was curious about this crown story and so she decided to leave them on standby as she asked Yonah, "What was the curse?"

"It was a *joke*..." Heydrich interrupted rather foolishly: the Subjects had learned many days ago not to speak unless they were Commanded to do so. Hitler made a small, frustrated grunt as though this wasn't the first time that the Hangman of Prague had been abrasive and stupid in the face of a God. Aliza was about to Command the Hangman to keep quiet when Yonah spoke again.

"The curse was that anyone who put on the crown and wasn't worthy of the Czech throne, any invader who tried that, he'd die within the year, and then his firstborn son would follow," the teen explained. "Year after Heydrich put on the crown, he got killed by Czech assassins."

"Coincidence," Aliza assumed, but Yonah shook his head.

"But then a year after *that*, his firstborn son died too. Got splattered by a bus while he was biking around his stolen mansion. The curse, that's what it was. Wenceslaus' spirit got his revenge on the invade—"

"What are you talking about?"

For a moment, the God of Nazi-Land was startled: she rarely allowed Heydrich to speak, and when he deigned to do so on his own before she thought to silence him, his tone was always one of absolute vitriol. She had never heard him sound...worried. She glanced at the Hangman and realized that he had stopped staring down at the carving on his arm and was gawking at the two Jews, lake blue eyes wide like a frightened puppy.

"Oh, ha! Himmler, you didn't tell him?" Yonah cackled, briefly glancing at Himmler as the Reichsführer clutched at his face and sobbed. Seeing that the chief of the SS was rather distracted by his own agony, Yonah rolled his eyes and smirked at Heydrich. "Yeah, asshole, your little baby boy got killed. I hear he was acting up because you weren't around. Ran out of the gate and got hit by a bus."

"You're lying." Heydrich's voice almost solidified back into its typical vicious tone, but there was a fearful note to it. Aliza realized that for once, the Hangman was trembling even though she was no longer Commanding him.

"Nope, not me!" Yonah continued. "One year after you died. Heard it from one of the slaves who was forced to work on your property. And the brat didn't even die right away. It took *hours*. Little baby Heydrich Junior was choking on his own blood, probably crying for Papa."

"You're lying…" Now the vitriol was gone, replaced by a sort of desperation that was too familiar to Aliza. She had seen it at the orphanage before Amos had come for her and Heidi, when fathers and mothers came looking for their children and only ever found heartbreak.

Aliza hadn't even realized that Heydrich had children. Actually, she hadn't thought about any of her Subjects' families. Not their children, or their parents, or anything of the sort. If they had families, she would have thought that they would regard their spouses and children as mere objects at best and punching bags at worst. Monsters didn't love anything, after all.

Aliza had seen Heydrich cry before. She had made him cry many times. She hadn't thought that she would ever see him cry for his child. It made her gut twist. She hated seeing a face that she despised take on a look that was familiar and human.

"That's real karma, you know, after all the kids you killed. Only injustice is that you weren't there to see it," Yonah declared, which might have made Aliza nod in agreement and harden her heart with another reminder of *an eye for an eye* if the teen hadn't then turned to his partner with a smile.

"Hey, Liza, you know, you could *make him* see it," Yonah noted. "Take away his memory, make him forget he's in Hell, put him right in that moment. You're a God, after all. You can make up any scenario you want."

Heydrich let out a choking noise, and Aliza felt her heart jump into her throat at the thought. Yes, of course, Aliza *could* do something like that. She actually hadn't thought of it before since she considered herself a direct person, wont to punch someone she didn't like rather than play mind games, but it was well within her power.

She could make the Nazis forget that they were dead. She could create whatever situation she wanted with only a few words. She could make them watch their loved ones die and suffer over and over.

She *could.* But the thought of doing so was making her gut twist. She hadn't before because she hadn't even considered the fact that monsters such as these had loved ones they would mourn, that making them experience such a thing would be more torturous than making them hit themselves or break their own bones.

"You're only trying to get a rise out of me, damn Jews!" Heydrich cried, as helpless as he was furious, tears streaming down his face. He gripped his dagger with both hands and pointed the tip of the blade towards his own heart, as though he wanted nothing more than to receive another Command to carve it out. That would surely be preferable to watching his son die.

He deserved to watch his son die. Aliza could make him watch his son die. In fact, she could do worse than that. She could make him shoot his own son. Make Hitler beat his own mother to death. Make Goering crush his daughter's skull. Make Goebbels poison his own children over and over and over…

"Looks like it's wooorking!" Yonah chirped. "Liza, c'mon, make him—!"

"Enough! ***Heydrich, stop crying and shut up!***"

Heydrich did, the tears ceasing to flow even as he watched the two Masters with frightened anticipation.

Aliza didn't want to make them kill and torture their loved ones. Not because it was too much, not because they didn't deserve it, but because she hated to see them cry from heartache. The thought that they even *had* loved ones was making her nauseous. She would rather leave the Zone forever than be reminded that these monsters were human.

"Don't ask him questions anymore without my permission, and don't tell me what to do with my Subjects," Aliza snapped, rising from her seat and scowling not at her Subjects, but at Yonah. "*Ever.*"

For a moment, Yonah scowled and opened his mouth, apparently ready to argue, but then he must have remembered that he was merely a powerless Invader in Zone N-1. Berating the God of Nazi-Land would certainly not end well. "O-okay…" he muttered with a shrug. "I like direct methods anyway."

Aliza nodded curtly, and with a few words, she healed her Subjects' wounds, rendering them bloody but whole, ready for a future round of torment. Heydrich quickly turned around, refusing to face the Master now that he had some modicum of freedom. She saw him lift his now-healed arm to wipe at his face.

Hitler was staring at her, striking blue eyes unblinking and filled with curiosity. Aliza suddenly felt like vomiting, and for once, she wanted to get out of the Zone as quickly as possible. "I'm done for the day! C'mon!" she decreed, and Yonah quickly followed her back into the Master Room.

———— ▽ ————

The Subjects of Zone N-1 had learned from the boy who tended to trail their sixth Master that the girl's name was "Liza." This was more than they had known about their last Master, whose name had been an utter mystery and whose presence they were actually beginning to miss. True, Master Five had been horrendously, viciously vengeful, but his cruelty had bounds. He had never Commanded this much, and for some time under his reign, the Nazis had even experienced a period of relative reprieve when he had ceased tormenting them.

They experienced a brief period of reprieve after "Liza" and her little boyfriend exited. In her haste, she had not frozen them with a Command before she left or made sure to shut them in an Iron Maiden overnight, and so they were allowed a moment to catch their breaths and talk.

"Talk" being a relative term. It was mostly crying, Himmler being the loudest of them all as he sat on the floor in a pool of his own blood.

"I can't take this, I can't take this!" wailed the man who had damned millions of people to death with a smile. "I'm not built for this! I'm not! I can't take another moment of this, much less an eternity!"

"None of us can!" Goebbels cried, half snarling, half sobbing. "Nobody is built for this! I would have thought we would have all gone mad by now, but we can't even escape that way!"

"Heydrich, are you all right?" Goering inquired, mopping the tears from his pudgy face and waddling over to the Hangman of Prague, who was being uncharacteristically still. Typically, Heydrich spent their rare breaks searching about their Zone, hoping to find some sort of hole or crack that they could possibly use to escape this corner of Hell. Now, however, Heydrich was sitting on one bloodstained chair, staring down at the dagger in his hands, not crying, but also making no attempt to wipe the dried tears and blood from his face.

"Is *he* all right?! *None* of us are all right, Goering!" bleated Goebbels, but Himmler, who realized what Goering was really asking, sat up slightly and adjusted his shattered pince-nez glasses, peering at his old underling's face.

"Reinhard?" he said, and Heydrich let out a small grunt as though he had been jabbed in the gut.

"They were telling the truth?" he said. Himmler bit his lip and nodded, rising from the crimson puddle on the floor.

"Did he die slowly, and in pain?" the Hangman asked, and Himmler held up both hands and shook his head.

"N-no, it was very fast, I mean I…"

Heydrich gave his superior a glare that he had once reserved for Jews who found themselves in the jail cells of Gestapo HQ. *"Don't. Lie."*

Himmler, weak by nature, found that when he couldn't lie, he couldn't speak at all. He could only whip off his bloody, broken glasses and nervously fiddle with them, which for Heydrich, who knew his boss' habits well, was enough of an answer.

"You should have told me," Heydrich said, accusatory tone barely masking his sorrow, and Himmler let out a noise like a chicken getting its throat slit.

"Why? To upset you?!" the *Reichsführer* cried. "You're already in Hell, why would I want to make it worse when it doesn't even make a difference?!"

"H-Heydrich," Goebbels interrupted, and for once, the Nazi who always spoke with flawless confidence bumbled, stumbled, and stuttered. "I know it's a tragedy, but if you think about it, it's a good thing. The poor boy didn't have to grow up in a world without National Social-ism, a world ruled by Jews like those *monsters*. I mean, if that's only two of them, can you imagine what the world looks like since they won the war?! Klaus didn't have to—"

Goebbels was cut off as Heydrich gave him a glare worthy of a Master at their most vengeful. The propagandist made a noise not dissimilar to the one that he had let out when the Master had forced him to bite off his own tongue.

"Goebbels," Goering grunted, wrinkling his nose at the Nazi propagandist. "Just because you thought that killing your children was a swell idea doesn't mean everyone agrees."

The few parts of Goebbels' face that weren't already covered in blood turned scarlet. He hopped to his feet, stomping his bad foot and screeching in rage. "Just because *you* were so *disloyal* that you tried to lay all the blame at *our* feet when you were on trial at Nuremberg—!"

"That is *not* what happened! Master Five *lied* about that!" interrupted Goering. "I was willing to go down with the ship like the rest of us, I simply wasn't willing to tie an anchor around my daughter's legs while I was at it!"

"And I wonder what she's doing now!" Goebbels cried, his tone as desperate as it was furious, trying at once to comfort himself for his own choices and make Goering fearfully question his. "I'm sure Edda is *perfectly safe* and *happy* in whatever *hellscape* that Europe turned into once the Jews took control!"

Goering, for a brief moment, seemed to let the thought that his daughter was suffering up on Earth get to him as he winced, but then the *Reichmarshall* shook his head and glowered at his comrade. "I'm not going to have my parenting choices critiqued by *you* of all people, Goebbels."

"*Me of all people*, you have a lot of—!"

"Enough! All of you, *silence!*"

Adolf Hitler had been adapt at making his ever-squabbling underlings be quiet in life, and while he was no longer the master of his own soul, the Subjects of Zone N-1 had always found it difficult to break from the habit of obeying his orders.

They all looked towards the Führer as he stood before a cracked mirror and wiped his hand across his face. He was covered in his own blood, and his equally bloody hands did little more than make him even filthier. Grunting in ire, Hitler contented himself to brush his mop of dark brown hair back into place before turning to face his fellow sinners.

"What exactly is this arguing supposed to resolve?" Hitler inquired, letting his bright blue eyes, which were even more striking when contrasted against the crimson blood covering every inch of his body, flit from Nazi to Nazi before they settled on the Hangman of Prague. "And you, Heydrich, this is no time for mourning! I need you to think clearly right now."

"I'm thinking clearly," Heydrich said, bristling a bit. The Subjects generally tended to fall into line and do what Hitler said, but Heydrich was always the one who fussed about doing so the most. Hitler decided to ignore his underling's petulant tone and strutted to the center of the room, arms behind his back, posture straight, remembering to appear in control even when he wasn't.

"Good," the deceased Führer declared. "Because this situation is intolerable. This Jewess is awful enough on her own, and now she's got that little sadist boyfriend of hers feeding her medieval ideas. Even the last Master gave us moments of reprieve, and he eventually stopped using Commands all together. This Jewess, however, is a complete monster. She needs to go. Nothing that could replace her could be worse."

"I wouldn't bet on that...but I agree," Goering

mumbled, massaging his neck and glancing at the now intact piano. Goebbels, forgetting about Goering completely, looked to his leader like a dog desperate for his owner's comfort during a thunderstorm.

"My Führer, you're right, of course, but what can we possibly do!?" the propagandist yelped. "She's a God here! She can do whatever she wants with but a word! We can't lay a finger on her!"

"She'll just do what she did previously and summon a shield," Goering noted.

"It's hopeless!" Himmler wailed, and Hitler grunted, fidgeting with the Iron Cross pinned to his chest.

"Perhaps," the Führer mused before he let his gaze return to Heydrich and gestured to the blade in the SS man's hand. "But consider what she said about that dagger."

Heydrich looked down at the blood-covered blade and held it up a bit. "My dagger," he said, and Hitler nodded.

"Precisely. *Your* dagger. Not merely a dagger that she created with her powers. She called it an 'Artifact' and said that she got it during the Fox Farm Incident. When she makes you stab yourself with it, does it feel any different?"

"Hurts more than typical daggers," Heydrich mumbled, and Hitler's eyes glowed with eagerness.

"I thought so!" the dictator declared, becoming energized with hope. He gesticulated wildly as he spoke, pointing from Heydrich's blade to the Master Room. "I suspect that the dagger may have some property which differentiates it from the things that the Master creates down here. Perhaps if we could hit her with that dagger before she Commands us, she wouldn't be able to defend against it since it's not something that she herself made!"

"That's assuming she loosens her grip on us long enough that we can even *try* to hit her," Goering muttered, and Hitler nodded, punching his open palm with one tight fist.

"It is a long shot, but we certainly don't have anything to lose," the Führer declared. "Everyone, when you see an opening, talk to the Master, distract her, take her attention off of Heydrich. Heydrich, when you get the opportunity to kill her, *don't hesitate.*"

Heydrich gripped the hilt of his dagger tightly and wiped the tears from his face.

"Don't worry," the Hangman vowed. "I won't."

"ALL RIGHT, LADIES AND GENTLEMEN, REMEMBER THAT WE do not have class on Monday. Enjoy Purim with your families, and be ready for a quiz on Wednesday."

The class let out a massive groan of protest at the notion that they would have to study during their holiday vacation. Nonetheless, as they filed out of Miss Miller's homeroom, the students were generally in good spirits. Aliza, however, had missed the announcement and would have been left behind if not for her sister.

"Liza, wake up! C'mon, class is over," Heidi said, her tone one of utter frustration as she shook her sister awake. Aliza emerged from the Zone with a grumble and cast a scowl at Yonah when he snickered at her on his way out the door. Aliza still wasn't sure why he never seemed to go down to his Zone when he was in class. Maybe cautious-ness, or maybe because he still had fun causing chaos in the classroom.

Either way, the duo didn't meet in Zone N-1 except at night or in the treehouse. She didn't want to accidentally strand a powerless Yonah in Nazi-Land if her sister woke her up in class: evidently, he couldn't leave Hell except from his own Zone. Of course, if he gave her an attitude, she might consider briefly leaving him in Zone N-1 one day. Scare some respect into him.

"Miss Auman!"

"Yes?" Both Aliza and Heidi spoke in unison. Miss Miller let out a frustrated grunt and pointed to Aliza with her red pen. "You, stay. Heidi, go. *Chag Purim Sameach*."

"*Chag Purim Sameach*," muttered Heidi, not even sparing a glance at her sister as she marched out of the classroom. Aliza huffed and shoved her useless textbooks into her bag, slowly trudging towards her teacher's desk. She hated this, hated feeling powerless when infinite power was in her hands. She hated feeling like a Subject in the real world when she was a God in the afterlife.

Aliza stood before her teacher's desk, refusing to hide her disdain or let her scowl morph into a pleasant smile like she would have in the past. Miss Miller and Aliza exchanged glares for a moment before the teacher sighed and pushed a paper towards the teenager.

"Your last exam," Miller said. Aliza only spared the sheet a brief glance, and she hated how the sight of a bold scarlet "*F*" still made her heart sink. She despised being at the mercy of another person.

"Do you have an explanation for this? Or the last few quizzes?" Miss Miller said, her voice as cold as Heydrich's was whenever the God of Nazi-Land let him get a word out. Aliza wanted to tell Miss Miller to shut her mouth, but she *couldn't*, and that made her bristle.

"No. I'm not a good student, I guess," Aliza declared with a shrug.

"That isn't true," declared Miller, tapping her long painted nails on the desk. Every *tap, tap, tap* made Aliza's head throb and made her feel like the Contract on her chest was burning.

"You were maintaining a 'C' average. You have *never* previously failed a test or a quiz," declared Miss Miller. "I notice that all of this started several weeks ago, since you became close to Yonah Meckler."

"My friends aren't your businesses, and Yonah isn't—"

"Yonah isn't a good student, but he *does* at least maintain a passing grade point average, so I don't think this is *exclusively* his influence," Miller interrupted sharply before she bit her lip, sighed heavily, and folded her hands on the desk. She leaned forward and spoke in the most horrendously patronizing tone, the tone that she no doubt used for her cats when they scratched at the furniture. "I want to know what's going on, Miss Auman. I want to know if something is going on at home, or with Yonah, or with your health. I can offer some leeway if you're earnest with me, but I can't be merciful if you simply brush me off."

Merciful! Fury consumed Aliza's heart. "I don't need to tell you anything, you bitch!" she snapped before she could stop herself, stomping her foot and screaming like one of the younger children of Beth-Hadasha, the ones who hadn't endured hunger and cold, who hadn't learned that tantrums could be deadly. Even Yonah had never outright cursed at Miller, and the old lady was clearly taken aback. Her thin lips parted in shock and her eyes widened so much that they seemingly expanded past the borders of her glasses.

A small part of Aliza's soul immediately chastised her, begging her to apologize right away. Her father could get in trouble if she misbehaved, after all, and even if that didn't happen, Miller had been nice enough to offer leniency even though she didn't have to. She really didn't deserve such vicious disrespect.

But Gods didn't apologize, and so Aliza didn't even give Miss Miller a chance to recover from her shock. The God of Nazi-Land turned on her heel and stomped out of the classroom.

───────── ▽ ─────────

"She chewed ya out, huh?"

"She's *such* a bitch."

"Yep."

"I don't even think it fucking matters. English class! Totally useless!"

"Hey!" Yonah yelped with feigned umbrage, gesturing to his uncompleted manuscript. Aliza, who had called dibs on his sleeping mat, laid back on the slightly cushioned surface and shook her head.

"You don't do your English assignments," she said, and Yonah shrugged.

"Not most of the time, but I try to *pass,*" he said, patting his manuscript like it was a beloved pet. "I think a publisher wouldn't like it if I submitted a manuscript and had to explain that I failed outta English."

"Whatever," sighed Aliza, staring up at the planet and star stickers on the ceiling and trying to discern if Yonah had bothered to form actual constellations on his treehouse roof. "I don't need English."

"You don't need *anything,* really. You don't even need a job. You could just stay in the Zone all day if ya wanted. I mean, you can eat and drink in there. Just gotta find a nice hole where nobody'll bother you and bury yourself alive," Yonah noted, which fetched a chuckle from Aliza.

"Sounds nice."

"Hey, seriously, though, what *do* you wanna be?" Yonah inquired, sounding genuinely curious. Aliza hesitated for a moment before deciding to be earnest.

"I always wanted to be a cop," she muttered. Long before she had ever become a warden of the afterlife, she had enjoyed the idea of serving society as a policewoman. She could have a uniform, a gun, and the right to fight against the evil bastards of society, the mini

Hitlers and Heydrichs of the general populace. Aliza had loved the idea of decking a child murderer right in the face with a baton. It would have been great: power plus righteousness, the same feeling that the Contract offered.

Aliza mentally readied herself for Yonah's inevitable disparagement. In the past, any time she had told someone about her desire to be a cop, she'd been met with ridicule and misogyny at worst. At best, she would be given a gentle laugh and a, "Sure, sweetie." Amos was always supportive of his daughters and their interests, and he certainly knew that women could be very effective fighters since he always talked about his female friends from the Black Foxes, but even he had discouraged Aliza from becoming a police officer simply because it was too dangerous.

When Yonah replied, however, it wasn't with a sneer and a roll of his eyes, but with excitement. "A cop! Yeah, I think you'd make a good cop!"

That made Aliza's heart do a cartwheel. She sat up on her elbows, looking at Yonah with surprise. "Ya think?"

"Uh huh, definitely," the boy declared, and Aliza felt her face burn.

"Might be hard," she said, collapsing onto the sleeping mat again and scowling up at the fake stars. "Most police academies won't accept girls. I could probably be a guard at a women's prison, but that's it. Blagh. Maybe I *will* just bury myself alive and be a Master forever."

"Hey, c'mon, don't," Yonah said, his voice becoming gentle, genuine. "Your dad and your sisters would miss ya. And I'd miss ya, too."

Aliza looked at her partner again and saw that his cheeks were strawberry-scarlet. Silence, utterly awkward and unbearable, descended upon the two blushing teens before Aliza resolved to kill it quickly. She sat up, grabbed the Black-Sun Brotherhood's poster, and threw it onto the floor.

"Uh! I was thinking!" she cried. "Purim's coming up, which means the march is coming up! The assholes in Nazi-Land didn't know shit, so maybe we shouldn't go down today or we'll get distracted. We should just brainstorm right here and see what we can come up with!"

"R-right!" Yonah agreed, nodding hastily "Let's get creative!"

Aliza dearly wanted to go down into the Zone. Being treated like a powerless little girl by Miss Miller made her nearly desperate to cement her status as a God. Nevertheless, the only thing she hated more than feeling powerless was Nazis, and she realized that if she procrastinated any longer, she would have to feel powerless in front of an entire parade of the bastards.

She helped Yonah lay out every document that he had gathered about the parade: the papers that talked about Nicholas Jackson, the articles about the legal drama behind the planned march, the poster that had been plastered on the Beth-Hadasha synagogue.

"So..,Jackson used to be in the US military, and it seems like he only turned into a Nazi after he served in the Second World War," Aliza observed, jabbing her thumb at one article. "The Black-Sun Brotherhood existed during the war as an isolationist pro-Nazi movement, but when America entered the war, they dissolved. Black-Sun Brotherhood pops back up a few years after the war with a new chief, and now they've made arrangements to march through Beth-Hadasha because they know it'll provoke us."

"When they were arguing in front of the Supreme Court, the Black-Sun Brotherhood claimed that they're not intentionally trying to harass the residents of Beth-Hadasha," Yonah said, pointing towards the poster advertising the march, "They say they're just 'memorializing' the 'real Holocaust' against the Germans.''

"Yeah, what's with that?" Aliza said, pinching the corner of the paper and pulling it towards herself. *"'Hamburg, Dresden, Brennenbach, the real Holocaust…'"*

"They're referencing the bombings," Yonah declared with a sneer. "Goebbels did the same shit during the war, said that the Allies were the *real* war criminals because they *dared* to bomb German cities even though the Germans had been bombing London and Warsaw for years. Ha!"

Yonah took the paper from Aliza and stared down at the proclamation with a bitter smirk decorating his face. "And I dunno about Dresden and Hamburg, but I can tell ya for a fact that Brennenbach deserved to be firebombed into Hell."

"Never even heard of the place," Aliza said with a shrug, and Yonah started nervously raking a calloused hand through his untidy dark hair.

"Small village. There was a little concentration camp there run by a piece of shit named Rahm." Yonah tapped the Contract glistening on his chest. "They made guns for the Axis…or, you know, made *Jews* make guns for the Axis. Shipped any Jews that they couldn't use to Auschwitz and Treblinka. My first Contract was for the Nazis from Brennenbach."

"Your first…were…you there?" Aliza asked. "At the Brennenbach camp?"

"Thankfully, no, or I'd be a crisp right now since the Allied bombs didn't exactly spare the Jews and smoke the fascists." Yonah sighed, glancing at his pile of books, his eyes landing on a copy of *War of the Worlds*. "No, I had a bone to pick with Rahm's troop. Before they were trans-ferred to Brennenbach, they were just a gang of Jew hunters who went from place to place, sniffing out Jews who hadn't been deported. Jews who were hiding. Rahm's troop found me and my mom...and...my dad...and my little sister."

Aliza felt her heart freeze. "I didn't know you had a sister."

"*Had* a sister." Yonah looked away from the books and up at the star stickers on his ceiling.

"Did Rahm...?"

"Not himself, no," Yonah said, shaking his head. "But he and his men found us, arrested us, shipped us off. We ended up in Terezin. My sister died on the way there in the cattle car. My dad got shot one day. I dunno why. We just found his body outside in the snow. Guess there doesn't have to be a *why*, though."

Briefly, Yonah touched the Contract on his chest before he spoke again, his tone hushed. "Me and Mom survived Terezin, but we eventually got put on a train to… somewhere. Auschwitz, maybe Treblinka. But then the Black Foxes blew up the rail track. Saved us. Mom was pretty much ready to die by then, though."

Yonah's eyes shifted to the clumsily cut-out window on the treehouse, and he softly whispered, "I think she's still ready to die…"

There was deathly silence between the two teens for a moment before Yonah let his gaze shift from the window down to his chest, to the Contract above his heart.

"The Brennenbach Contract was my first Contract," he explained, tracing the triangle with one finger. "Been spending the last two years making those bastards pay for what they did to my family. The fact that anyone's trying to *mourn* those assholes..."

"Do you think we could use the Brennenbach Contract?" Aliza suggested, gesturing to the poster before them, and Yonah shook his head.

"Nah ah. No more than we could use N-1."

"Maybe we could fight fire with fire? Show pictures of the Brennenbach camp, show *why* they got bombed?"

"That shit doesn't matter. Nazis don't care about the truth; they just care about perception."

"Perception. Yeah…these Nazis only care about perception…" Aliza mumbled, her gaze flitting from the poster to Hitler's Contract as she recalled something Miss Miller had said. *They just want a reaction. Any reaction.*

But that was wrong, because there was one type of reaction that Nazis never enjoyed: laughter.

"They care about being either the poor victims of the evil Jews, or the strong Germans triumphing over the weak undesirables," declared Aliza. "They've pinned us into a corner so that either one of those becomes the perception, but what if we add a third option? Make this parade into a total joke."

"Joke...hm…" Yonah stroked his chin, his scowl slowly morphing into a hopeful smile. "Hitler always *did* hate it when people joked about him."

"He *still* hates it," Aliza noted. "He hates being humiliated, and Heydrich too—they hate it when we see them cry and scream. They hate it when I Command them to act like idiots. We can't Command the Black-Sun Brotherhood, but we *can* embarrass them."

"That's a good idea. And if we do that, they'd definitely never wanna come back to Beth-Hadasha! And it'd give everyone in town a laugh instead of a reason to be afraid," Yonah exclaimed, regarding Aliza with a look of such overwhelming admiration that she felt her face heat up again. "Okay, so...what can *we* do to make this a—?"

"Aliza! Aliza Auman!"

"Yonah, you little shit, you get your ass down here!"

"Miss Meckler, *please!* Aliza!"

Both Aliza and Yonah grimaced in unison as two adult voices called out to them, one in a gently chastising tone, the other in a snarl that shook the whole treehouse. The teenagers crawled to the window and looked down.

At the foot of the tree were both of their respective parents. Miss Meckler, wrapped in a stained bathrobe, glared up at her son with murky, red rimmed eyes. Amos' gaze shifted from the drunk woman at his side to his daughter. With one finger, he beckoned for Aliza to come down.

Yonah, for his part, crawled back over to the sleeping mat and offered his partner a sympathetic smile as she started towards the thatch.

"Your mom...?" Aliza started to say, and Yonah sighed.

"Forget it," he said. "She'll give up and go back in. Talk to ya later, Liza."

"*Chag Purim Sameach*," she muttered, giving her fellow Master a small nod and crawling down the ladder.

She leapt down onto the ground and briefly glanced at Miss Meckler. It seemed that Yonah's declaration that his mother would give up quickly was spot-on as the woman muttered something about queers and then turned on her heel, stumbling into her home. Amos waited until Miss Meckler was well out of the way before he heaved an exhausted sigh, crossed his arms over his chest, and gazed down at his daughter with utmost disappointment.

"Your teacher called me," he said, and Aliza looked down at her dirty shoes so that she wouldn't have to endure his discontented expression. "She said you *cursed* at her today. Is that true?"

Aliza grunted in response.

"Aliza, this is *serious*."

"So what if I did?" Aliza grumbled, fiddling with one of the buttons on her shirt and scowling down at the glistening Contract above her heart. She could feel it thrum in tune with her pounding heartbeat.

"Aliza Auman, there is *no* reason to curse at a teacher,

especially not when she was only trying to help you!" Amos declared. "I'm fine with you spending time with friends and classmates, but not if it gets in the way of your schoolwork, and certainly not if you're going to act like this!"

"Yonah didn't have anything to do with this!" Aliza hissed, and she heard her father let out a concerned hum.

"If *he* didn't, then..." Amos' eyes flitted to the Contract, and finally, Aliza looked up.

"It wasn't that either!" she insisted. "I just got mad, that's all!"

"That *isn't* an excuse," Amos declared, and Aliza almost winced. Amos never shouted at his girls no matter how mad they drove him. He wasn't yelling now, but he was using a forceful tone that she was sure she'd only heard him use thrice in her entire life. "You *know* there's no excuse for that behavior, and you're lucky that I managed to smooth-talk Miller into not expelling you for that! As it were, you're grounded for the next three weeks. Straight home from school, no Yonah visits, no going anywhere but school and synagogue."

"You can't do that!" Aliza screamed, curling her hands into fists and suddenly feeling that weighty sensation of oppression and powerlessness. Her father reached out and grabbed her wrist.

"I can, and I am, and you're lucky that I'm not taking away your *extracurriculars* too!" he declared, glancing briefly down at the Contract. "Now *we are going home!*"

Amos began to drag her away from the treehouse, and a combination of humiliation and anger overwhelmed Aliza. It wasn't fair. She wasn't a little baby girl that could be ordered around. She wasn't a helpless little child that needed to obey *or else.*

"Get off!" she screeched, fighting her father as he started yanking her away from the Meckler residence.

"You're not even my real dad! You can't order me around like this!"

The words had barely escaped her mouth when she felt a bolt of guilt strike her heart. Amos' grip on her wrist briefly slackened, and the look that he gave her, one of genuine pain, made her throat tighten. A part of her wanted to apologize right away, but pride and the power of the Contract held her back. Gods didn't apologize.

Amos let silence reign between them for a moment, perhaps hoping that his scowling daughter would recant that hastily, indignantly delivered statement. When she merely kept her eyes pinned on the ground, he let out a sigh of defeat.

"Nevertheless," Amos said. "I'm still your guardian, and you're still grounded. We're going home."

Aliza nodded, keeping her head bowed as she allowed Amos to lead her home, refusing to spare a look back at the treehouse. She could still speak to Yonah via the Zones. A God could easily overcome a grounding, but the guilt strangling her chest as pride refused to let her apologize, that was a different hurdle entirely.

PURIM HAD ONCE BEEN ALIZA AND HEIDI'S FAVORITE holiday. The Jewish festival which celebrated the biblical tale of the beautiful Queen Esther and her defeat of the faintly Hitlerian Haman was a favorite among many folks in Beth-Hadasha. The annual Purim celebrations in town were always raucous. Children dressed as characters from the Esther tale, and plays about the Jewish Queen were performed practically all day.

Normally, the Aumans, Samuel, and Aunt Ava, who always came by to visit on Purim, would have a meal at Amos' house and then join the rest of town in partying the night away. The children would play games and gorge themselves on candies. The adults, religiously mandated to drink until they were plastered, would obey God's will until their livers nearly gave out.

Aliza had been looking forward to enjoying Purim as an adult since she was too old to play dress-up (Heidi was too, but that hadn't stopped her since she insisted on wearing a little tiara anyway.) Unfortunately, the God of Nazi-Land was grounded, and so she shut herself in her and Heidi's room, alone.

The sound of her sisters giggling happily, having fun without her, made a toxic swill rise up in Aliza's chest. She was angry, and while a part of her wanted to go right down into Zone N-1 and give Hitler a particularly brutal bout of torture to celebrate the holiday, something kept her planted on Earth. That weighty feeling of guilt. She didn't hear her father's cheerful laugh echoing about the household.

Knock! Knock! Knock!

"Liza?"

She sat upright, her heart leaping into her throat. "Come in, Dad!"

Aliza heard the hefty sigh of relief that Amos let out upon being called 'Dad' even through the door. He entered the room and carefully parted Aliza's curtain, offering his daughter a small, gentle smile.

"Not Zoning out?" he said, and she shook her head.

"Perfect day for it," Amos observed, and Aliza sighed.

"I'm just…y'know…" the girl mumbled with a shrug. "Thinking."

"About?"

"About…stuff."

"Ah, very particular, demon girl. The thing I love about you the most is your descriptiveness."

That fetched a chuckle from Aliza before she bit her

lip and looked down at the Contract, tracing it with her finger.

"Can I come down for dinner, at least?" she mumbled, clutching at her growling stomach.

"Grounding doesn't mean starving, sweetie," Amos said. "You were always welcome to come down. I wasn't sure you *wanted* to come down."

"I wanna say hi to Aunt Ava and Uncle Sam, at least."

"Come on, then. I'll even let you drink a glass of wine. No going out to party, though."

"The party part's for little kids anyway," Aliza said, sliding off her bed and following her father out of her room.

"Little kids and adults," Amos noted. "Teens get the short end of the stick until they're old enough to *really* drink."

"No fair."

"Nothing in life is fair, sweetie. Only death is fair." Amos turned around and tapped the Contract on his breast, and Aliza giggled. Before they could enter the sitting room, however, guilt forced her to grab her father by the arm and pull him back.

"Ah, I didn't...I mean..." Aliza muttered clumsily, gazing down at her wrinkled slacks as shame weighed down her gut and turned her tongue into a pretzel. "I didn't mean when I was..."

Amos saved her by patting her cheek. "I know, hun. Don't worry about it. *Chag Purim Sameach.*"

Aliza looked up, took comfort from the forgiving smile Amos offered, and declared, "*Chag Purim Sameach.*"

"I think you've missed most of Sam's story by now," Amos said. "He's already at the midway point."

Indeed, when Aliza arrived in the living room, she found that her sisters and Otto Keller, Aunt Ava's son, were all sitting around Samuel as he recited the tale of

Queen Esther from memory. Samuel held Uta in his lap and didn't pause the tale when he saw Aliza, but he did spare a smile and a wink at the teenager as she crossed the room and scurried to where Aunt Ava sat.

Ava Keller was one of Amos and Samuel's old friends from their time in the Black Foxes. A lovely, cheerful lady who always carried with her the aura of a woman who had climbed to the peak of a mountaintop, whose trials and tribulations were over.

She was a slim lady, quite in shape thanks to her love of gymnastics, with shoulder-length dark hair and shimmering night-black eyes. She wore a black dress that perfectly matched her eyes and enough makeup to accentuate her features without caking it on like Heidi tended to. She was a real lady, but also rather tough. Aliza had picked up most of the swear words she knew from Ava.

"Hiya, Aunt Ava," Aliza greeted in a hushed whisper, not wanting to interrupt Samuel's story. She embraced her aunt, and Ava returned the hug with tender strength. Aliza and her family didn't see Ava too often since the Kellers were rather reclusive, living somewhere in the countryside, but even though Aliza didn't see Ava as often as she saw Sam, she still felt connected to her. Ava never greeted the Auman girls as strangers even when they spent the year separated.

"Hey, sweetie!" Ava chirped. *"Chag Purim Sameach."*

"Your husband didn't come?"

"Nope, not this year!"

"Not any year," Aliza noted. Amos and Sam continuously insisted that both Aliza and Heidi had met Ava's other half several times, but Aliza didn't recall the occasion. She frankly didn't even remember the name of Ava's husband, much less his face. He was even more reclusive than Ava, and apparently always "working." It put Aliza a bit on edge, and she could only hope that there was an innocent explanation for the fact that Ava's husband was eternally absent.

Of course, if Ava's husband had a mistress, he would have to contend with Aliza, Sam, and Ava all wanting to kill him. If he was wise, then he really was a workaholic.

Ava laughed nervously, which didn't do much to assuage Aliza's feelings towards her aunt's husband, and gave the girl a small push towards Samuel. "Go sit with your sister. I think Otto's driving her crazy. She'll be thankful for a human shield."

Aliza turned and saw that Ava's seven-year-old son was indeed tormenting poor Heidi: Otto had grabbed a lock of Heidi's long hair and was tugging on it mercilessly. Snorting, Aliza nodded.

"I'll save her," she vowed, leaving her aunt with her father while she tip-toed over to Otto and her sister.

"Hey, squirt, move over or else," Aliza threatened, giving Otto a tap on the shoulder. The little boy whined and bleated something about girls being mean before he relented, knowing full well that Aliza could and would put him in a crushing headlock if he didn't obey.

"You're welcome," Aliza declared once Otto retreated to the floor. She plopped down beside her sister. Heidi adjusted her tiara and sighed, shrugging.

"Uh, hey, I'm here?" Aliza said, waving a hand in front of her sister's face. Heidi grunted and shoved her hand aside.

"I see you, shush! I'm listening," she snapped, gesturing to Uncle Sam. Aliza might have argued with her sister or tried to bully her into giving a proper "thank you." Her attention, however, was captured by her uncle when she realized that he was reciting one of her favorite chapters of the Esther story: the part where Haman was utterly humiliated after King Xerxes commanded him to dress his Jewish enemy Mordechai up in silken robes and parade him through the city on a royal stallion.

"At the King's command," Samuel recited, his voice, usually quiet and clipped, taking on a strength that rivalled that of Rabbi Eliezer. "Haman gripped the horse by the reins and led Mordechai through the streets of the great Persian capital, crying aloud, 'Make way for the King's friend and hero!' At that moment, Haman's eldest daughter peeked her head out from the topmost floor of his great manor and saw the procession. Thinking that her father was on the stallion, and it was Mordecai the Jew leading the horse, the girl ran to get her chamber pot—Uta, what's a chamber pot?'"

"Neigh!" replied Uta, who had decided to dress as Xerxes' horse for Purim. The adults all chuckled with charmed amusement.

Shaina, who had gone the more traditional route by dressing up as Queen Esther, raised her hand. "Uncle, Uncle! I know!" she cried, and when she was called upon, Shaina declared, "It's like an ancient potty!"

"That's correct!" Samuel said. "It's where people used to go pee. She grabbed the pot full of pee and ran to the balcony, then tipped it over..."

"Oh no!" squealed Uta. "Yuck, yuck!"

Otto laughed. "And then Haman got peed on!"

"He was *soaked*, Otto," Samuel assured the boy. "And certainly not very happy. Completely humiliated."

The children giggled, and while Samuel assured Uta that the horse had not been splashed by any pee when Haman had a chamber pot dumped on his head, Aliza's eyes sparkled. Haman, the original Hitler. Haman humiliated...

"That's it..." she whispered, smiling widely before leaning back and shutting her eyes. Quickly, Aliza delved into the Zone, intent on running to the Looking Glass and calling for Yonah. She didn't even get the chance to leap off of the silver throne, however; she felt a harsh tug and suddenly, Aliza was back on the couch, being shaken awake by her sister.

"Liza! Liza, for God's sake!" Heidi was whispering. "You're so rude!"

"Can you stop?" Aliza hissed, elbowing her sister in the gut and causing Heidi's tiara to nearly topple off her head. "I'm just shutting my eyes for a minute, leave me alone!"

Aliza attempted to lie back and enter the Zone again, somewhat afraid that the idea would slip from her mind if she didn't quickly deliver it to Yonah, but Heidi shook her again, rough and insistent and *annoying*.

"You've been sleeping all day, and you were sleeping all day yesterday too!" Heidi snapped.

"Get off!" Aliza said, slapping Heidi's hand. Heidi let out a yelp of pain that was perhaps too much for the light tap she'd been dealt, but it got everyone's attention. Sam stopped telling the story, Ava winced, Amos let out a huff.

"Girls—!" he started to say, but Heidi unleashed a hiss of anger and smacked Aliza's arm. Heidi was frail and the hit didn't hurt at all, but it was obnoxious enough to make Aliza jump to her feet and push her sister away. The tiara flew off of Heidi's head and landed behind the couch, nearly hitting poor Slowpoke's box.

"Don't be such a bitch!" Aliza shouted.

"Bitch!" Otto squeaked cheerfully, and Ava's face flushed red. She quickly grabbed her son and instructed him not to say that word.

"Aliza, language!" Amos cried, but the girls were too wrapped up in their own argument to even hear their father chastising them.

"You're the one being a bitch!" Heidi cried. "You hit me first! And you were falling asleep and being rude!"

"There's nothing rude about falling asleep!"

"You could at least *pretend* that you wanna be with your family instead of your stupid boyfriend!" Heidi spat the word *boyfriend* with utmost vitriol, and Aliza felt a flush of embarrassment creep up to her cheeks. She was about to deny being Yonah's girlfriend, but Heidi kept *talking*.

"If you weren't grounded, you'd be with him right now, wouldn't you?" the blonde girl snapped.

"Yeah, maybe!" Aliza snarled.

"You've been such an asshole since you started hanging out with him!" Heidi cried, and if Aliza were less annoyed, then she might have heard the slight wobble in her sister's voice and recognized how upset she was. But Aliza was aggrieved and angry, and she didn't even consider comforting her sister.

"Who I hang out with *isn't* your business!"

"It is when you're with the guy that's been calling me a Nazi every day for a year!"

"Well, maybe he's got a point 'cause you act like one!"

Shaina and Otto, who didn't know any better, snickered at that. But every adult in the Auman household stopped breathing.

"Uncle?" Uta said, glancing worriedly at Samuel as he gawked at his niece, slack-jawed. Aliza huffed, glowering down at her sister. Heidi's made-up face looked like one of the Russian dolls on the mantlepiece: eyes and mouth perfectly circular.

And then she started crying. No, not crying. *Bawling.* Whatever God was occupied with in Heaven, even He would have likely needed to put it aside to see what the ruckus was about, so loud were her cries.

Aliza's scowl melted into an expression of horror, because Heidi had cried before, but the last time she had cried this hard had been when the two of them had different surnames. When they met, when Heidi had lost her mother and Aliza had hugged her fellow prisoner, not caring at all whose daughter she was.

Aliza hated remembering that moment, because she loved her sister and hated remembering her gut-wrenching sobs. Because she hated Hitler and Goebbels and Heydrich for making Heidi cry so terribly. Because she remembered the feeling of powerlessness that had consumed her as she'd wrapped her little arms around Heidi and tried to make her stop crying, knowing that there was nothing she could do to actually *fix* it.

And now she had made Heidi cry just as horribly, and that realization made a gut-churning sensation fill Aliza's stomach. She didn't want to be here. She wanted to leave.

She almost dove into the Zone right then just to escape it all. Instead, she ran upstairs, ducked behind the curtain, and fell upon her bed, clutching her Contract-covered heart and trying to make the guilt go away. A part of her wanted to go down into Hell so she could torture Hitler and the others, but right then she realized that she couldn't. She couldn't stand to look at them knowing that they now had something in common, even something so small.

"Aliza." She heard her father open their door. Grabbing her duvet, Aliza threw it over her head like she was a little girl again, hiding from shadows and nightmares.

"Aliza, come down and apologize to your sister." It was difficult to imagine that Amos Auman was able to use Commands when even this was not an order, but a plea.

Aliza hated what she had done, but Gods didn't apologize. And besides, she didn't want to look at Heidi right then.

"Aliza…"

"I'll make it up to her later," Aliza vowed. She heard her father unleash a great sigh before he shut the door and left her alone with her thoughts and plans.

Chapter
SEVEN

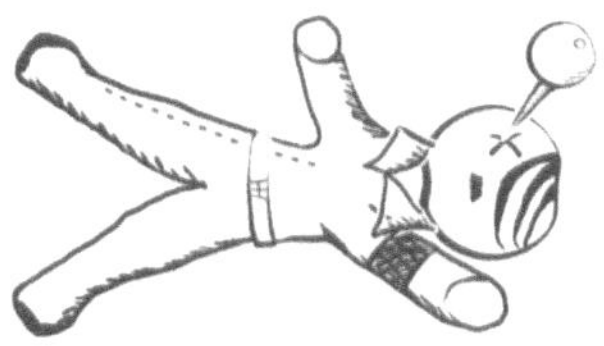

The day of the Black-Sun Brotherhood's march arrived, and the citizens of Beth-Hadasha needed to make a choice: fight or flight, at least metaphorically speaking. Many of the civilians chose to duck into their houses, shut the blinds, turn on the radio or the TV as loudly as possible, and do their best to pretend that the Neo-Nazis did not exist.

Some, however, decided that they had hidden from the Nazis once before, and they weren't going to hide again. Amos Auman fell into this latter category.

"Girls are inside?" Sam said, meeting Amos on his front porch as he exited his house, locking his door behind him. Amos offered his friend a small smile before heaving a sigh.

"Heidi's watching Uta and Shaina," he explained, jabbing his thumb towards his front door. "Aliza was snappy today, ran out. Pretty sure she's with Yonah Meckler. She's supposed to be grounded, but I just don't have the energy to argue with her today. Hopefully, she won't try anything stupid."

"Hopefully," Sam concurred, shifting his weight and checking to make sure that the hammer he had brought along was safely secured to his belt. Of course, he didn't intend on starting anything, but if the Nazis did, well, he planned on letting his dormant Black Fox out of its cage.

"You're sure you want to do this?" Samuel inquired as he and Amos started walking away from the Aumans' abode. "You don't have to..."

"Yes, I do," said Amos firmly, and Sam dropped it right then. He knew that his friend had spent too long in hiding: hiding in a barn, then on a farmhouse, then ducking and covering with armies of orphans and refugees that he had been in charge of smuggling to safety as Black Fox 860. Amos had done more than enough hiding for one lifetime.

Rabbi Eliezer had lined up the people who would be counter-protesting. He instructed them to say *Kaddish* for their family members, and if they didn't wish to pray, he told them to say the names of the ones that they had lost. A few people were holding up pictures of their children, parents, or spouses that had been stolen by Hitler's regime. Those were the lucky ones: Sam and Amos didn't have any pictures.

"Here, just stand a little behind me," Sam said as he and Amos took their places on the sidewalk. Amos would have normally chastised his friend for still treating him like a baby brother even after all of these years, but right then he was more than happy that the tall Russian was there to protect him. The Neo-Nazis weren't visible yet, but he could already hear their chants of, "No more Jew lies!"

The Black-Sun Brotherhood rounded the corner: they were a rather motley lot of about thirty men. They stomped down the street not in a straight, orderly line, but in a slightly crooked oval.

The man who marched at the forefront of the blob of

Nazis was the motliest of his crew: Nicholas Jackson was balding, short, and pudgy. If Aliza had chosen to make some demented chimera of Goering and Goebbels, the result of such an experiment would have likely resembled the chief of the Black-Sun Brotherhood. As he led his disordered, bristling men down the street, Jackson raised up a hand and offered a Nazi salute, barking "Sig Heil!"

His butchery of the German language may have been funny in different circumstances. As it were, while the gang marching down the street bore little resemblance to the well-groomed battalions of the SS, the sight of men carrying swastika banners and signs plastered in anti-Semitic slogans was enough to make many of the Jews begin to sob. Some fell silent as shock and terror made them quiver. The Rabbi kept on praying even as he clutched at the number sewn onto his forearm.

"Amos…?" whispered Samuel in concern, keeping one hand on the handle of his hammer and glancing at his friend. Amos' turquoise eyes were pinned not on the swastika banners or Jackson himself, but on one particular Nazi that was carrying a large sign.

THE REAL HOLOCAUST: BRENNENBACH!

Beneath that scarlet proclamation, the sign showed off a picture of a bombed-out town filled with ragged survivors sitting on chunks of rubble, crying or nursing burns.

"Amos, you're fine," Samuel said, patting his friend on the shoulder. Amos took in a sharp breath and nodded even as tears started filling his eyes. Jackson looked at the Jews quaking and crying, and an ugly sneer stretched across his face as he gestured for his followers to march past the synagogue, towards the counter-protestors.

But just as the Nazis began to cross in front of the

synagogue, the speakers dotting Beth-Hadasha crackled to life. The PA system which was supposed to send out announcements about the weather or warn the civilians of incoming nuclear annihilation instead began to belch out a zany tune.

"Venn the Führer says, 'Ve ist the Master Race!' Ve Heil! Heil! Right in ze Führer's face!"

An old anti-Nazi propaganda tune featuring silly trumpets and a goofy German accent. Amos recognized it right away and realized who the culprit had to be. The song was *Der Führer's Face*, and the culprit must have been Aliza, who had loved that tune ever since she had heard it in a Donald Duck cartoon from the war.

The Neo-Nazis' sneers turned into expressions of flustered horror, and the Jews' sorrowful determination fractured as several counter-protestors began to laugh.

"Wha...where is that...?" Jackson snapped, but he was cut off as a window on the topmost story of the synagogue opened and the Nazis were suddenly assaulted with a flurry of water balloons. The Nazis ducked and covered, but several were struck, and the yellow fluid that covered them...

"Ugh!" one of them yelped, dropping his stained swastika banner and tearing his soaked shirt off. "Fucking kikes are tossing piss at us!"

The laughter of Beth-Hadasha's Jews became uproarious. Several people who had been hiding in their homes peeked past their curtains and joined in the raucous laughter when they saw that the Neo-Nazis were scattering, flailing, and blubbering with disgust as water balloons full of urine rained down upon them, the continued loop of *Der Führer's Face* barely masking their cries of umbrage. One of the Nazis started stomping towards the synagogue, but Jackson grabbed his arm and pulled him back.

"No, you moron, we can't touch property or *we'll* get

in trouble!" Jackson snapped. "Everyone clear out…and you lying kikes!"

Jackson pointed a chubby, accusatory finger at the Rabbi, who was practically blind from the tears of laughter streaming down his face. "This is intentionally disrupting our constitutionally protected march and when we find out who did it, we'll…!"

But Jackson was cut off as the mysterious piss-balloon thrower nailed him right on the head. He let out a yelp of disgust, and with that, he and the rest of the Neo-Nazis scattered, dropping their piss-covered banners and signs, all but tripping over themselves to escape this horrible, humiliating situation.

The Jews of Beth-Hadasha cheered as the Nazis bolted. Amos looked like he was about to die of laugher: he knelt on the sidewalk, clutching his sides and gasping.

"This is the best day of my life!" he announced, and Sam, never one to break down laughing but nevertheless cracking an uncharacteristically large smile, nodded.

"Quite the turn around. I have a feeling…" Sam's keen eyes flitted to the far-off backyard of the synagogue, and he spotted a small figure leaping the fence, confirming his suspicion.

"Hey, stay here, okay?" Sam said since it seemed that Amos wouldn't be able to stand up anytime soon. "Don't break a rib. I'm gonna go make sure the kids are okay, make sure nobody hurts them."

"All right! It *was* Liza, then?" cackled Amos. "Tell her I love her so much, she's my favorite daughter for the week! For the year!"

"Too bad nobody'll be able to celebrate her, or you'd get sued into destitution," sighed Sam, patting his friend's shoulder and setting off after the retreating shadow of Aliza Auman.

▽

Aliza stopped outside the radio tower, pausing to catch her breath and rest her arms, which were stiff from tossing so many piss balloons (she had to admire Yonah for his ability to drink so much water in such a short amount of time.)

Speaking of which, Yonah popped out of the back door of the radio tower, sporting a giant grin as he slid down the arm rail and leapt in front of her. "Well?" he prodded, and Aliza burst into laughter.

"It was great!" she gasped before recounting what had happened. Aliza felt rather bad that Yonah hadn't gotten to see the Neo-Nazis get so thoroughly humiliated, but one of them had needed to temporarily take over Beth-Hadasha's PA system, and Yonah, who researched gadgetry often for his novel, had declared that he would be the best person for the job.

Yonah certainly didn't seem upset at only being offered a second-hand account of their operation's success. He cackled happily and then gave a deep bow towards his partner. "All hail Aliza, genius God of Nazi-Land, defeater of the Black-Sun Brotherhood!" he cried.

"Give my uncle credit for giving me half the idea and letting me 'borrow' the keys to the radio station," Aliza laughed, thankful that her uncle happened to fix radios for a living and had a maintenance key for the tower on him at all times. She would have to return it later. "Then while you're at it, thank my dad for giving me the Contract. Wouldn't have gotten the inspiration without it."

"No shit!" laughed Yonah. "Ha-Satan didn't pick you, then?"

"Nope. Dad gave it to me. He figured I could use it better than he could."

"Well, he was right!" declared Yonah. "You're so good at humiliating Nazis, you can do it on Earth too!"

"You're just being nice so I'll keep letting you come by and kick Hitler's ass even though the treaty's concluded," Aliza snickered, and while she spoke in a jesting tone, her statement made Yonah's smile vanish on the spot.

"Something wrong?" Aliza asked, and Yonah began to almost frantically comb his hand through his curly hair. His face was red as a tomato, and he seemed physically incapable of looking Aliza in the eye as he spoke, instead staring down at the dusty ground.

"Well...uhm...being honest, if we could keep being...you know, partners...that'd be nice..." Yonah said, stuttering and bumbling, so obviously lovesick.

It was cute. He was cute. Aliza knew when she was beaten, but she let him flail about a little more.

"Uhm...I *am* sorry about your sister, like I said, I was just being an asshole because I was working through shit, and, and, if you want me to really apologize, I'll do that. Uhm…I…uhm...I like you...working *with you*...uh…"

"You're stuttering like an idiot." Aliza sighed at last when she decided that leaving him like this for another moment would be cruel even for her. "Wanna date?"

She hadn't thought that it would be physically possible for Yonah to turn redder, but somehow he managed, shaking worse than Hitler did when he was Commanded. "D-d-d-date?" the teen stuttered before nodding eagerly. "Uhhhhh...yeah, I do."

"Great," Aliza said, giving Yonah a light punch on the arm before she leaned forward and kissed his cheek.

"I, ahhhhhhh...oooookay," Yonah said, half yelping, half singing, clutching his chest as though he was about to collapse from a heart attack. "I'm gonna diiiiie..."

"Don't die!" Aliza commanded with a giggle. "I think you're the only boy who's ever liked me."

"I've liked you for a while, uh...you're different," Yonah confessed, bowing his head and wringing his hands. "Ah...shit, shit, okay, I was kind of just expecting you to punch me and call me an idiot. Now you wanna date and I dunno what to do. Uh…you wouldn't like flowers, would you?"

Aliza wrinkled her nose and stuck out her tongue.

"Okay...uhm. Date, then," Yonah muttered, twiddling his thumbs and staring thoughtfully down at his dusty boots. "Uuuuuh, what should we do? And what should I bring instead of flowers? Bugs? Lizards?"

"Bring me a book on Viking torture methods," Aliza said, and that made a very cute smile bloom on Yonah's face.

"I can get that!" he declared. "The bookshop owner's used to me buying weird shit for researching my novel. I bet she won't even bat an eye."

"Meet tomorrow?" offered Aliza. "At the treehouse?"

"Treehouse, yes! Treehouse date! Date at the treehouse!"

"I'm gonna run home and check on my dad and sisters, make sure they're happy with how it all went down!" announced Aliza. She bade farewell to Yonah with a punch on the arm and another kiss on the cheek that sent him into a tizzy.

Unfortunately for her, Samuel Val had been standing behind a nearby gate, listening, and neither blushing teenager had noticed him bolt towards Aliza's house.

Chapter
EIGHT

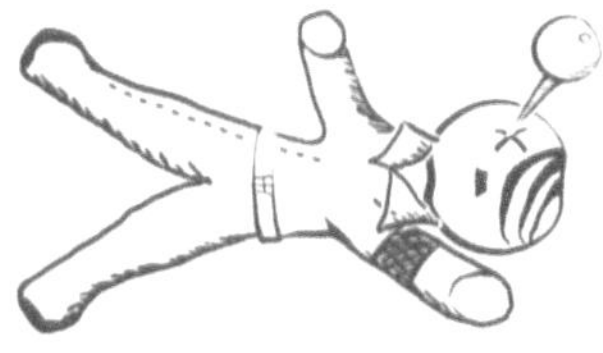

"Liza, hey!"

Aliza was rather surprised when, as she reached her cul-de-sac, she found her sisters walking down the street. Heidi held both of their younger sisters' hands.

"Hey, Heidi, Uta, Shaina," Aliza said. Uta greeted her with a cheetah growl, having switched her favorite animal again. Shaina giggled.

"The Nazis got covered in pee," the junior gymnast said, and Aliza chuckled.

"Yep, I saw."

"You *did*. Is *that* what you and Yonah were plotting?" Heidi inquired. Her tone was rather cold, but Aliza noticed that the edge of her sister's mouth was twitching as though a part of her would have liked to smile if pride were not preventing it.

"Yup! Worth it?" Aliza asked, and the smile that Heidi had been fighting against lost the war as a grim expression consumed her face.

"No," Heidi said. "You're gonna have to do better than that."

Aliza grunted and pouted at her sister's inflexibility, but she decided not to argue on this day of victory. "Where are you three going?"

"To Miss Devorah's house," squeaked Shaina. "Uncle Sam kicked us out!"

"Kicked you out?" repeated Aliza, lifting a brow and glancing past Heidi's shoulder at her house.

"He looked mad. He was growly! Rawr!" Uta declared, and that made Aliza shake her head in disbelief. Frosty as Samuel was, he rarely seemed to actually get angry enough that the girls would have noticed his mood.

Curious and concerned, Aliza gestured for her sisters to continue on to their destination. "I'll catch up," she said. "Gotta grab something at home."

"Okay," sighed Heidi, her eyes softening a bit. "Just, uh, knock. He *did* look really mad."

"Don't worry about me," Aliza said, patting Uta and Shaina's heads and smiling at Heidi. "See ya later, ladies."

"I'm a cheetah, not a lady!" Uta insisted. Shaina bade farewell to her sister while Heidi offered a small nod and dragged the younger Auman girls towards Miss Devorah's house.

Aliza arrived at her home and found that one of the windows was wide open. Trying her best not to trample Heidi and Amos' precious plants, she crept into the garden and squatted under the window, listening closely.

"...How the *fuck* did you even know where it was!?"

That was definitely Sam's voice, though Sam was always so cool-headed that Aliza didn't recognize it for a moment: her uncle was screaming, and cursing too, which the religious man *never* did.

She peeked into the house. Her dad sat on the couch, elbows resting on his knees, head bowed, brow subtly pinched as though he was fighting off a headache. Samuel, red in the face, was pacing back and forth in front of Amos, huffing like a furious bull being teased by a matador.

"I knew that you must have hidden it in one of the holy books so that Ha-Satan couldn't touch it," sighed Amos, lifting his gaze and chewing on the inside of his cheek. "Angels can't disturb holy books."

"But how…?"

"Book of Yonah. Easy. The part where he gets swallowed by a whale." Amos' tone took on a hopefully jocular note, as though something about that statement was supposed to force his friend to laugh.

It didn't work. Sam let out a snarl of rage and kicked the nearby bookshelf. Aliza pitied poor Slowpoke, whose enclosure trembled.

"I can't believe you!" snapped Samuel. "You *stole* the Contract!"

"You weren't using it!" Amos argued, and Aliza had never heard her ever-patient father sound so utterly annoyed. Sam spun about. For a brief moment, Aliza shivered as her uncle's familiar eyes took on a ferocity identical to the sort that Hitler usually offered his Master.

"You *know* why I wasn't using it!" Samuel barked, and Amos huffed and shook his head.

"I really don't! You just came up to me one day shivering and said that you were gonna renounce the Contract, and when I said I'd take it, you panicked and started screaming that nobody should ever have it."

"I renounced the Contract because having it, using it, using *Commands*, it gave me the same feeling that I felt when I nearly killed Heidi!"

What?

For about two seconds, all Aliza could hear was her own internal denial. *What? No, no, that's not…what?* Confusion battered her brain. Uncle Sam almost killed Heidi? She didn't remember anything like that happening in the Fox Farm. No, Sam had *saved* Heidi. He loved Heidi, and Heidi loved him. Heidi wouldn't have hidden something like that from her sister, so it must have been something that even Heidi herself didn't remember.

"That's *different…*" Amos said, and Aliza shook her head and listened close, hoping that her father or uncle would unwittingly offer her some sort of explanation.

"*Oy, meyn Gott!*" Samuel exclaimed, throwing his hands into the air. He turned on his heel and walked away from Amos, towards the mantle, staring at the wax-covered menorah that acted as its centerpiece. Amos rose to his feet, and now when he spoke, there was actual anger in his voice.

"It is! It's *different!*" Amos insisted. "Heidi's an innocent little girl who just happened to be the daughter of an insane war criminal! By keeping the Contract hidden for this long, you've let *Adolf Hitler* and *Reinhard Heydrich* off the hook! They've just been sitting down there, twiddling their thumbs, not getting punished for what they did! You think using Commands is wrong? *That's* wrong!"

"Really? *Really?*" Samuel snapped, spinning around and clutching at the fabric of his shirt, at the area right above his heart where the Contract would have been had he not relinquished it. "So, you think an eternity of *soul-rape* is a perfectly acceptable form of punishment!"

"Stop calling it that!" Aliza's chest ached as Amos all but shrieked that demand.

"That's what it is!" Sam insisted. "Don't pretend like that's not the *reason* you use it! *Ain takhat ain*, an eye for an eye! Just like I used to think…"

Samuel's anger petered into something else. His shoulders sagged, he clutched his heart tighter, and he looked down at the floor, shivering like a beaten dog. Amos' eyes softened for a moment, and he stepped towards his friend, reaching out briefly before his turquoise eyes darted down and landed upon his own Contract. Curling his outstretched hand into a fist, Amos drew back, touching the Contract above his heart.

"He deserves it…" Amos whispered, and Aliza felt like an arrow of ice had pierced her heart. She had never heard her father speak like that, in such a harsh tone. Samuel looked up, and once again, there was fire in his bright blue eyes.

"You think so?" he said. "And Hitler? And Heydrich? And *all* the rest of them."

"Sam…"

"*Nazis* deserve to be Commanded, huh?"

"Sam, don't you dare go there…"

"What about your Nazi *boyfriend*, hm? Does Franz Keidel deserve to be soul-raped for all eternity?"

What? What? What? What?

A torrent of confusion and shock overwhelmed Aliza's brain so thoroughly that only a truly strange sound could drag her out of it. That sound was Amos Auman shouting in rage.

"How dare you even *suggest* that Franz is in Hell?!" Amos screamed, and she had never seen her father like this: face contorted in fury, hands folded into trembling fists. Sam himself seemed taken aback for a second, but he held his ground and responded in kind: with an indignant yell.

"Because he almost certainly is! Franz might have saved your life, but he was a *Nazi*!"

"Franz was *different*!" Amos insisted, and Sam slammed a fist against the nearest wall.

"*No, he wasn't!*" Samuel shouted, striking the wall thrice more as though to emphasize his every word. "Stop pretending that he redeemed himself! Stop pretending that he's waiting for you in Heaven!"

"Franz was a good man!" Amos' voice was breaking from anger and sorrow. Aliza briefly saw his eyes flit to the bookshelf.

"He was a murderous piece of shit!" Samuel decreed, and Amos' gaze returned to the Russian, utterly affronted.

"He saved your life!" Amos cried.

"Because he wanted me to free you, you, *you!*" Samuel cried, closing the distance between himself and Amos, jabbing an accusatory finger at his friend's chest. "And then what did he do *after* I freed you? He went on to serve as a *guard in a concentration camp*! I may not like the Contract system, but I'll tell you what: I'll always regret that when I stabbed that piece of shit, I didn't send him to Hell right then!"

Slap!

Aliza almost gave herself away by letting out a squeak of shock when Amos' hand connected with Samuel's cheek, but neither man took note of her presence. Amos was a small, short man and Samuel was tall and used to much worse. The Russian didn't even touch his cheek, merely grunting once before casting a scowl at Amos, who was red in the face.

"Out, out! Get out of my house right now!" screamed Amos, tears spilling from his eyes as he pointed towards the front door.

"Gladly," snapped Sam, elbowing his friend on his way out the door. "Have fun being a God, Amos!"

Aliza felt her heart leap into her throat. She squatted down again, hoping that the tall flowers and the darkness of night would conceal her. It apparently did. Sam walked straight past her and started marching towards his home, spewing Yiddish curses as he did so.

Aliza was conflicted for a moment: she could hear

her father sobbing inside, and part of her wanted nothing more than to run in and embrace him, but that conversation had contained too many strange revelations. She needed answers first, and her father likely wouldn't provide them, at least not until he had calmed down.

Aliza crept out of her family's garden and followed her bristling uncle.

SAMUEL VAL LIVED IN A SMALL TOWNHOUSE ONLY TWENTY minutes away from the Auman household. He wasn't a materialistic man, having few possessions to his name, and so it must have taken very little time for him to pack his things. Aliza arrived at his home and stood outside on his front porch step. Samuel swiftly emerged from his house with one suitcase in hand and winced when he nearly bumped into her.

"Aliza," he said, pausing to put down his suitcase and lock his front door before turning to the teenager. "Good, I was hoping to…"

"I heard you talking with my dad," Aliza said, crossing her arms over her chest. "What's this about a 'Nazi boyfriend'?"

Her uncle offered an expression of utter horror: his already pale face became white as a sheet of paper, and briefly, his eyes widened. Samuel's gaze then became severe as he dropped to one knee and grabbed the girl's shoulders tight.

"Listen to me, Aliza Auman," he whispered in a tone that was deathly serious and distinctly familiar. Perhaps her first father had used the same tone when warning Aliza not to make a sound lest the Nazis find them. "I don't approve of your father's choices, his homosexuality, I *don't.* But he is a good man, and he does love you. You can't…"

"I don't care about that!" Aliza huffed. It was most certainly a surprise, though not entirely shocking. It explained why her father had always been so accepting of her tomboyishness. She herself had been called a dyke so often that she had half a mind to make it her middle name even if the epithet was entirely inaccurate.

She was glad that it *was* inaccurate. If she *had* been queer, she would have needed to dress different, dress *normal,* act less like a girl with nothing to hide. The Jews of Beth-Hadasha had spent time in camps and ghettos alongside homosexuals, but that alone couldn't wipe away old prejudices, and even if it had, that wouldn't have mattered in the eyes of the state.

Amos had already attracted quite a few raised eyebrows for being a single man with four adopted daughters. Rumors had once been spread accusing him of being a homosexual, but he had quashed those by dating nearly every woman in his workplace.

And it was a good thing he had, because if anyone learned that Amos was queer, he would be lucky to get away with his life. He would certainly lose his job: nobody would want a queer man near their children. He would *definitely* lose his daughters.

Aliza was, frankly, shocked that her religious uncle apparently knew Amos' secret and hadn't tried to stone him to death. Then again, Samuel also knew what would have happened to Amos and his children if he was forced from the closet. He apparently loved his friend enough to put his own beliefs aside and keep his secret for him. Aliza couldn't help but feel a small wave of gratitude towards her uncle.

Samuel let out a sigh of relief and patted her shoulder.

"Good…good. You must swear to *Adonai* that you won't tell a soul for as long as you live."

"Swear to *Adonai*," Aliza declared, placing a hand over the Contract and almost shivering as she felt it *thrum, thrum, thrum.*

"Good girl…" Samuel's shoulders noticeably relaxed, and she offered him a gentle smile. If it weren't for the myriad of questions she had, she might have hugged him right then. Instead, Aliza spoke again.

"Uncle, you said he was a *Nazi*, though. What did you mean by that?"

Samuel let out another sigh and shook his head. "That isn't for me to say, sweetie."

"But—"

"If Amos wants to tell you, let him. But it's *his* private story. I think if you tell him what you just told me, though, he'll be happy to share."

Aliza chewed on her tongue, narrowed her dark eyes, and crossed her arms over her chest. "All right…what about what *you* said about Heidi? That's your story, so it *is* yours to share."

Briefly, another look of horror passed over Sam's face before a grimly resigned expression took its place and he gestured to the stone staircase leading up to his front step.

"Sit," he said, and Aliza did. Her uncle plopped down beside her, muttered a prayer to God, and then spoke: "You don't remember why Amos and I took note of you and Heidi in the Fox Farm, do you?"

Aliza shook her head.

"You don't remember that Amos talked to Heidi? That he mentioned he'd met her mother?"

"I…don't remember that," Aliza whispered. "But her mother was a Black Fox, that's why she was executed."

"Yes. Katja Naden. Black Fox Ten. I won't go into it too much…it is a long…*long* story…but her husband."

"Viktor Naden," Aliza muttered. The name tasted like poison on her tongue as she recalled the scarred stranger that had never reappeared after that initial encounter. "Heidi's…first father."

"The Beast of Belorussia," Samuel said, placing a hand above his heart and clutching at the fabric of his shirt. "I never told you this, but he burned down the village I come from. Khruvina. Killed my entire family. I was the sole survivor."

Aliza swallowed a lump. She had always assumed that her uncle's *shtetl* had been wiped off the map, but had never dared ask. You never asked someone what happened to their family in Beth-Hadasha, you simply assumed that they were ash.

"I'm sorry, Uncle."

She hadn't expected her eternally calm uncle to break down sobbing, but she equally hadn't anticipated the reaction he ended up giving her. Samuel stared down at the ground and his eyes…she shivered and touched her Contract, feeling the *thrum, thrum* of Hitler's soul.

"Well, I wasn't sorry at the time," Samuel hissed, his voice utter ice, exactly like Heydrich's on the rare occasions when the God of Nazi-Land let him speak. "I was *angry*."

"Right," Aliza said. "You should have been angry… but not at Heidi."

"I wasn't mad at her," Samuel explained, shaking his head. "You see, me and Amos were trying to get to safety at the time. Heidi's mother was the nearest Black Fox comrade we could run to. Of course, when I entered her house and realized this was Viktor Naden's family, I got…"

A shudder passed through his body, and his eyes became hollow and haunted. "Angry. *So* angry. I wanted revenge. To make Viktor Naden feel what I had felt. An eye for an eye."

"That's…"

"I tied up Heidi, her mother, and her sister. When Viktor Naden came home, I threatened to set them all on fire."

The thought was utterly inconceivable. Aliza knew her uncle. Her uncle was a good person who brought her Batman comics and called Heidi his *bubbeleh*. He would never hurt a little girl.

"You…" Aliza muttered. "Heidi…she's never mentioned this…"

"I'm sure she doesn't remember at all," Samuel assumed. "She was blindfolded at the time, and her mother was arrested and killed only a few weeks later. And she was so little…"

He looked up, eyes wide and devoid of fury now as fright consumed them. "Please don't tell her. I don't want her to hate me."

"I won't, Uncle," Aliza promised. Heidi deserved blissful ignorance. "You shouldn't feel bad. You're a good person, and you didn't hurt her."

"I *almost* did," Samuel said. "If Amos hadn't come in and snapped me out of it…"

Samuel clutched at his heart again, looking down at his hand and pausing for a moment before he whispered, "There was a feeling that took over me when I was holding a lighter above Heidi. I didn't even care about her. It was all about Naden, watching him get what he deserved and feeling powerful and *right* because of it. You know the feeling by now, Aliza."

Aliza grabbed at her own shirt, clutching the Contract. "That's not the same thing…"

"Isn't it, Master Six?"

Thrum, thrum. She could swear that it got faster, the

Contract's eternal beating, just as her heartbeat got faster and faster. "You almost hurt an innocent person," Aliza argued with not a small amount of anger.

"If you're cruel to those who deserve it, you'll eventually become cruel to those who do not," Samuel declared, facing her again, his tone resolute as a Rabbi reciting God's commandments. Aliza gritted her teeth and let her grip on the Contract slacken.

"You were the one who hid Hitler's Contract," she said, and Sam nodded.

"Ha-Satan was cross," the former God of Nazi-Land said. "Threatened me with an extra seven years in Purgatory if I didn't give it back. My mistake was telling Amos about it, but of course, he noticed that my Contract was missing and asked and he…just didn't *get it*."

"I don't either," Aliza admitted, shaking her head, and Samuel let out a bitter chuckle.

"I figured you wouldn't. And I know you won't listen to me, but I'm going to beg anyway: give up the Contract."

The mere thought instantly made nausea assault Aliza's guts. He may as well have suggested she chop off her leg. "I can't do that."

"That's the problem," Sam said. "You *can't*. You know, me and Hana, we…I haven't been very honest. We didn't part ways on the best of terms."

That made Aliza raise an eyebrow. She hadn't known Samuel's girlfriend very well, having only met her once or twice, but Hana had seemed like a lovely woman. Samuel always spoke so highly of her, but now his voice was consumed with regret as he glanced back at his suitcase.

"Every letter I've been writing has been an apology for the way I spoke to her, but she hasn't written back," he muttered. "When you Command once, Liza, you get used to it, so used to it that you won't be able to tolerate it when people won't just do what you say. The sort of power that the Contract gives you will make a good person bad and a bad person evil."

"Dad's had a Contract for years!" Aliza contended. "He's a good person!"

"Maybe he's just better than you or I," mused Sam half teasingly, massaging the cheek that Amos had slapped. "Really, though, I think Amos is just like Franz Keidel: he's good at compartmentalizing. He's sweet and kind to the people he loves, the people he thinks are *worthy* of kindness, but the people he hates? You haven't seen him when he's in Zone N-7."

Aliza bit her lip and squirmed, shaking her head. "I'm not…"

"I think you're a good person, sweetheart," Sam said, patting her shoulder briefly before his eyes became cloudy and he touched the spot above his heart again. "But every mother in Germany said the same thing."

Sam rose to his feet, standing over her, and Aliza suddenly felt like a tiny child again, listening to her wise Uncle Sam recite an old Yiddish saying. "The things we *know* about them are what they *thought* about us," the Russian declared. "'They deserve it.' Even if it's true, we still shouldn't. It has to *never* be okay."

Briefly, Aliza recalled what she had felt when Yonah had been teasing Heydrich about his dead son.

She banished those thoughts with a hefty dose of anger, by reminding herself of everything that had been taken from her. "That's total bullshit," Aliza snapped, and Samuel let out a disappointed sigh.

"That's your prerogative, then," he said, bending down and grabbing his suitcase. "My prerogative is to move on. I'll never forgive them, and I'd rather die than see them go to Heaven, but I also don't want to think about them anymore. I won't let them rule and ruin my life even when they're dead."

Samuel descended the stone staircase, then turned and gave Aliza a smile that was so terribly sad that it made her want to either vomit or run to him, hug him, beg him to stay. Pride and anger kept her planted in place, however.

"I have a train to catch," Sam said. "I'm going to DC, to apologize to Hana in person. Please, just think about what I said. I'm worried for you."

"I'll be fine," Aliza insisted. Samuel bit his lip, opened his mouth like he wanted to give another speech, but then he seemed to decide that he had already said all he could.

"Goodbye, Aliza."

She watched her uncle march off into the night, and once she was certain that he was gone, Aliza bolted home, her frantic heartbeat perfectly in sync with the *thrum* of the Contract.

Aliza arrived home to find her father sitting on the couch with a bottle of wine in his hand and a book in his lap.

"Honey, hi!" Amos cried, hastily putting the wine on the counter and shutting the book. It was Uta's copy of *White Fang*, the only book that Amos had refused to read to her for a bedtime story.

"S-sorry, honey, I'm still a bit upset about the march," he lied, hastily trying to wipe his tears away as he slapped on a smile. "Needed some alone time."

"Dad…"

"Your sisters are with Miss Devorah. I just called and they're having a great time! If you want, I can go upstairs, but they'd probably be really happy to…"

"Dad, I heard everything you and Uncle Sam said."

The mask slipped, the smile died, and for a moment Amos stared at her with utter terror in his eyes.

And then he started quaking, quietly sobbing. "I… I…" he stuttered, covering his face in his hands. "Please don't tell your sisters…please don't hate me…"

"Dad…" Aliza crossed the room in the blink of an eye and threw her arms around her father. Amos stiffened for a moment: he never liked being touched too suddenly, but he was typically always braced for a daughter to hug him. When his body relaxed, however, she could all but feel an entire lifetime's worth of weight lift off his shoulders.

"I don't care if you're queer, Dad," Aliza assured him. "Don't be stupid."

That fetched a wobbly chuckle from Amos, and he returned his daughter's embrace. "Sorry, hun. Stupid me."

She squeezed him tightly, and when she pulled away, Amos was still crying but smiling too. "I'm a little confused, though," Aliza confessed, sitting down on the couch beside her father. "You always date girls. I mean, you weren't just *pretending* to like Miss Devorah, were you?"

"Oh, no, no! I wouldn't do that to someone, I *do* like Miss Devorah!" Amos assured his daughter, hugging *White Fang* tightly to his chest. "I'm…oh, damn, I forget the term. I like both men and women."

"You were dumb to be that afraid of telling *me*." Aliza gestured down to her boyish clothes to emphasize her point, and Amos chuckled.

"I suppose you know all about being *different*, demon girl. I'll be honest: I always thought you might be the same until you started spending so much time with Yonah."

"I'd be more subtle," Aliza assured her father. "I won't tell Heidi or anyone else, don't worry. I doubt they'd hate you, though."

"You never know," Amos muttered sadly. "Even if they

weren't mad, Shaina couldn't keep a secret if her life depended on it, much less if *my* life depended on it."

Aliza snorted and nodded in agreement before she bit her lip and decided to broach the big and uncomfortable question. "Uhm…were you and Sam…?"

She tepidly touched the tips of her index fingers together, and Amos made a noise not dissimilar to the sort that Goering unleashed whenever she made him swallow one of his medals.

"No! Oh, no, no, no, goodness, no!" he blurted, laughing even though he sounded horrified by the mere concept. "We're just friends! Well…"

Amos looked down at the hand he had used to slap Sam and sadly whispered, "Maybe we *were* just friends…"

Despising the notion that Amos and Samuel would never speak again, Aliza blurted, "I followed him back to his home. He's heading to DC, to Miss Hana."

"And I bet he tried to get you to give up your Contract," Amos sighed. Aliza nodded.

"Yeah…funny thing is, he gave me my first Contract," Amos said. "He was the God of Nazi-Land before you were. The one who served for the longest amount of time, too. Ha-Satan was impressed with him, ended up giving him another Contract that was filled with old Ghetto Kommandants."

"Your Contract?"

"My *first* Contract. I'd rather not go into detail, but one of the Kommandants on the Contract was one that… hurt me. Badly. Sam knew about it. Gave me the Contract as a gift. I never would have been selected as a Master otherwise. Ha-Satan eventually ended up assigning me more Contracts, but *he* even said, 'I would have thought someone with your associations would be a bad fit.' Of course, he was talking about Franz."

"Franz. That's…uhm…the Nazi boyfriend that Sam mentioned, right?"

"Oh, he didn't tell you?"

"He said it was your private story, and I should ask you."

"That was nice of him…" Amos grumbled, scowling at the wall that Sam had punched. Aliza squirmed.

"If you don't wanna talk about it, Dad…"

"I sort of do," Amos confessed, running his fingers along the spine of *White Fang*. "I've always wanted to, but there's nobody to *really* talk about it with. Sam doesn't understand. Wine? Since I'm being a bad dad anyway…"

He offered Aliza the bottle he'd been drinking from, and she smiled, shaking her head. "You're not a bad dad. No wine for me, though. That's the shitty kind anyway."

"Basically grape juice. Sam always calls it an affront to God. Ah, well…"

Amos took a swig of the God-affronting wine, set the bottle on the table, and then held the *White Fang* book in front him, staring at the wolf-dog illustration on the cover.

"I won't get into too many gruesome details, but… when I was little, I had a neighbor my age. Franz Keidel was his name. We were best friends, he and I. We'd steal candy and play tennis and he'd try to save me from my cat when the little monster tried to attack me. He was…great. But he had a terrible father who blamed him for his mother's death. Beat him almost every day. Franz eventually couldn't stand it anymore. He ran away from home when he was a teenager without telling me. We didn't see each other again until the war started."

"He was your friend, but he became a Nazi…" Aliza muttered with confusion.

"He didn't know that I was Jewish. My family was much less Jewish than we are now," Amos explained, gesturing up to the menorah on the mantelpiece. "We didn't do any of the ceremonies, didn't even own a menorah. Wasn't something we cared about. But Hitler cared, oh, *he* cared…"

Amos briefly scowled at the Contract on Aliza's breast, at the little piece of Hitler's soul she held, before he shook his head and continued: "Franz was…damaged by what he went through with his father. He was a good boy, a good soul, but he was so…hurt and confused, he threw his lot in with the first man who told him that he had value. That man was Hitler. Franz joined the SS, served them hunting down Jews. Meanwhile, I was hiding with an old family friend. One day, Franz's troop came through. He stumbled across me. I thought he was going to shoot me, but he didn't."

Amos smiled softly, tracing the illustrated wolf-dog's face with his thumb. "He…saved me. Franz brought me food, clothes, books. He spent time with me, read to me. When my family friend found out that I was a queer, he refused to hide me anymore, but Franz took me to a different safehouse and started sheltering me. I thought he was just using me at first, but no…he just…loved me…"

Amos started to shake, his eyes filled with tears. "And I loved him too…I loved him so much…I wanted the war to be over so badly so we could just be together, find a nice farm, adopt some orphans, have a family and forget everything in the past…"

"Did…did the Nazis find out about Franz?"

"No, no. Thankfully, no. That would have been…*so* terrible." A shudder went through Amos' body. The treatment of queer men in the camps wasn't often discussed in Beth-Hadasha, but Aliza recalled from her time at the Fox Farm that any prisoner singled out as a homosexual had received particularly brutal treatment. If Franz's comrades had ever found out what he did, what he *was*, they would have been absolutely merciless.

"No, what happened was his troop was going to be moved," Amos said. "He couldn't take care of me anymore. He wanted me to be safe, and at the time, your Uncle Sam was being held in the prison at his headquarters. Franz and Sam staged an escape: Sam stabbed Franz, not lethally, but so that he could make it look like Franz had been attacked and overwhelmed."

"That's what he meant…Uncle Sam…" whispered Aliza, touching her stomach. "When he said he wished he'd…"

"Sam's always been…hostile towards Franz even though he saved both of our lives," Amos huffed. "He doesn't understand that Franz is *different*. But…back to the story. I went with Sam and joined the Black Foxes. Didn't want to sit back and do nothing, wanted to help kids, and…I was hoping that maybe, by chance, me and Franz would bump into each other again. The war came and went, and when it was over, before I went to get you and Heidi, I tried to track Franz down. I was hoping that we could all be a family together…"

The thought that she had almost had another father, and a former SS man at that, filled Aliza with a strange wave of both nausea and regret. Perhaps Sam had been right, and Franz Keidel had been no better than Heydrich or any of the other Subjects in Zone N-1, but on the other hand, if someone as sweet as Amos loved him, he must have been redeemable deep down.

"Luckily, Sam knew the unit Franz worked for," Amos said. "Franz's commanding officer was a man named Sigmund Rahm, and every man in Rahm's unit was transferred to a village called Brennenbach. Rahm was in charge of a little transit camp there. But…but…"

Amos' entire body trembled, and he clutched *White Fang* close to his heart. "Brennenbach got fire-bombed in 1944. The town was nearly completely destroyed, and there were no survivors at the camp. Every prisoner and guard that was in the camp that night died. Franz was on guard duty that night…he…"

Amos hastily took another drag of his drink, but he couldn't suppress the sob that tore from his throat. "Sorry, sorry, sweetie, I haven't really talked about this since the war ended…"

Aliza nodded numbly and barely heard Amos' next words over the buzzing echoes in her head.

…I had a bone to pick with Rahm's troop…

…Brennenbach Contract was my first Contract. Been spending the last two years making those bastards pay for what they did to my family…

"…I think it goes without saying that Sam is wrong. Franz was a good person. I *know* he's in a better place. I *know* that."

And Aliza could only suppress the frantic pounding of her heart, smile reassuringly at her sorrowful father, and hope that she was telling the truth when she said, "Yeah… yeah, Uncle Sam was definitely wrong."

Chapter NINE

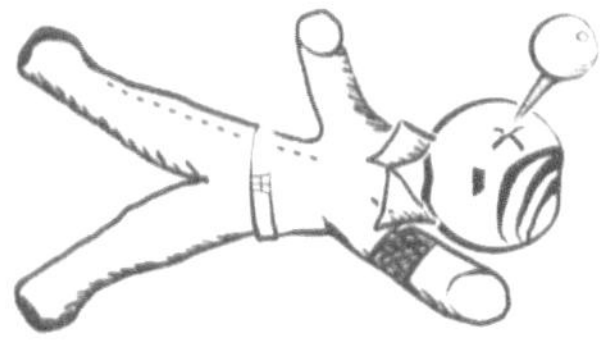

"Hey! Uhm, okay, so I couldn't find a book about Viking torture methods, but I did *find* one on Elizabethan..."

"Yeah, okay, cool, uhm, thanks!" Aliza blurted as she crawled into the treehouse and snatched the hardback from Yonah's hands, only giving the cover a brief glance and almost wincing when she saw a chair with spikes decorating the front of the book. She looked up at Yonah, who was blushing awfully. Good, good. If there was one thing she knew for certain, it was that boys would do whatever they could to impress a girl that they liked. She leaned close and kissed Yonah's cheek, which made him sputter adorably.

"Y-you're welcome!" he choked. If Aliza had possessed more feminine wiles, she may have waited, tried to build up to her request, but Aliza was eternally blunt and to the point.

"Uhm, hey, listen, remember how you said that you had the Contract with Rahm and all the Nazis from Brennenbach?"

"Er…yeah?" Yonah's flustered expression became one of confusion as Aliza held out her hand.

"Can I see it, really fast?" she asked.

"Errr, sure…" Yonah looked down at the golden triangle on his breast, and with but a thought, he summoned the Contract he desired to the top. He peeled it off and offered it to Aliza. The girl paused to set the heavy hardback on the floor and then took the Contract, hastily unfolding it.

"Is there a Nazi you wanted to punish? I thought you said you'd never even heard of Rahm," Yonah said, but Aliza paid him no mind, turning her back to the boy and scanning the names on the Contract with her eyes.

For a moment, Aliza thought that she would find nothing, that Sam truly was wrong, but then her pupils fell upon it: one little name, one cog in the machine of the Holocaust.

Franz Keidel

Her hands began to tremble as she clutched the golden paper holding a small part of Franz Keidel's soul. The soul of her father's first love. The soul of the man who had saved her father's life. He was a Nazi, yes, but she owed Franz Keidel every good thing that she had.

But he was in Hell, being tortured, having his will twisted against him just like she had been twisting Hitler's soul for the past few weeks. If Amos knew that Franz had been Commanded even once, he would be beyond devastated.

But Aliza had the power to save her father's beloved. She could reunite them. Perhaps together, she and Amos could even get Franz to repent of his sins, and then Amos wouldn't have to worry about his beloved's soul.

Mercy for mercy. An eye for an eye.

"I need this," Aliza declared, turning around and clutching Franz Keidel's Contract close to her own.

"Eh...what?" Yonah tilted his head sideways like a confused puppy.

"I need this Contract, Yonah."

"I heard what ya said, but I don't get why you need it," Yonah muttered with a slightly annoyed huff. "If there's someone down there you don't like, I could just invite you…"

"No, no, no!" Aliza cried, shaking her head, her heart palpitating at the thought of the man who had saved her father, the man that her father loved, being tormented. What had Yonah been doing to him? She could only hope that Franz Keidel had blended in with the crowd of monsters he had been damned with and hadn't drawn any special attention from the Master.

"Look," Aliza said, holding up the Contract and pointing to Franz's name. "I can't say very much, but this man right here, Franz Keidel, he's an old friend of my father. He saved my father and my Uncle Sam during the war. He saved them, and my dad doesn't even know he's in Hell, but he...he's *different*, get it? I *need* his Contract, please! I *owe* him."

Yonah lifted up a hand and gingerly took the Contract from Aliza's grasp. Aliza didn't know exactly what the process of transferring a Contract to another person looked like, but if Sam had given Amos one of his Contracts, then of course Yonah could do the same thing. He had other Contracts, after all, so giving up Franz's wouldn't cause him to lose his status as a Master.

"Franz Keidel..." muttered Yonah, staring down at the silver name. "Oh, yeah...*this* bastard..."

Aliza felt her heart drop. "You...know him?"

"I learned his name when I saw him on my first day with this Contract."

"Yonah..."

"Know *how* I remembered him?" Yonah hissed, raising his gaze from the Contract to Aliza. "He was one of the bastards that arrested me and my family. I remember how he grabbed my hair and pulled..."

Yonah was shaking, dark eyes blazing with anger. "I *never* forgot his face, the way he screamed, how scared I was."

"But...he…"

"He saved your dad. But he's one of the people who killed *my* dad. And clearly he didn't feel too bad about that or he wouldn't be on this."

Yonah turned the Contract around, showing off Keidel's name before releasing the paper. It folded itself back into a triangle and flew back onto the teen boy's heart. "So no offense, but I don't give a shit how much you owe him. I like you, Aliza. But I don't like you enough to give sanctuary to the people who killed my family. Keidel's getting *exactly* what he deserves."

"You...you can't do that," Aliza whispered, confusion and anger making her feel like her body was breaking apart.

"Of course I can," Yonah declared sharply, gesturing from Aliza's Contract to his own. "You're the God of Nazi-Land, but *I'm* the God of Zone N-56. It's *my* Zone. Franz Keidel is *my* Subject."

Yonah bent down, grabbed the book of Elizabethan torture methods, and showed off the spiked chair on the cover. "I can do whatever I want to him."

"You...you either give me the Contract or I'll never let you into Zone N-1 again!" Aliza cried, stomping her foot and making the treehouse tremble. She realized that she was acting childish, like a toddler that hadn't gotten what she wanted for Hannukah, but desperation and fury made her unable to control herself.

"Fine," Yonah said coolly, shaking his head and glancing briefly at the book pile, at his copy of *War of the Worlds*. "This is close to home."

"You'd rather torture Keidel than Hitler?!" Aliza exclaimed in disbelief.

Yonah chewed on his tongue for a moment, appearing to contemplate this question as he drummed his fingers on the hardback. He looked down at the book, then at the Contract on his breast, and then he shook his head.

"Y'know what? No. I'd rather torture Hitler," the boy declared. "So how about this: you give me the Contract to Zone N-1, and Franz Keidel's Contract is yours."

Aliza's pounding heart suddenly stopped. The inside of her mouth went dry for a moment, and when she spoke, it was in an accusatory rasp. "That's not a fair trade..."

"It is if saving your dad's friend really matters to you," Yonah said with a shrug. "More than fair, really. I'd be giving you the Brennenbach Contract knowing that you'd be giving leeway to one of the bastards who killed my family. You'd at least know that Hitler and the rest were still getting what they deserve, you just wouldn't be able to see it anymore. I couldn't let you in as a Guest or I'd risk you killing me when my back's turned and taking both Contracts."

"It's *Hitler*," Aliza hissed. "Hitler's a bigger fish than one little SS man...."

"He *is*. That's why I want him," Yonah said, pointing towards the book of Elizabethan torture methods before tucking it under his arm and nodding to the girl. "It's up to you."

Once again, Aliza was struck by the sensation that someone was tearing a limb off of her body. The mere concept of relinquishing the Contract to Zone N-1 made nausea fill her, nausea and the oppressive sense of power-lessness.

Desperate for a chance to win, to keep both, she remembered what the Master Manual had said and blurted, "Fight me for it."

"What?"

"Fight me for it! Let's have a Master Battle!" Aliza demanded, confident as she was in her own skills. If she could knock Yonah to the ground on Earth, then surely she could do the same thing in the Zone. Even if she lost, at least she would go down swinging, not giving in. "We can even have it in your Zone! The best fighter gets all the Contracts!"

She had thought that Yonah would smirk at that. Commend her for her spirit and agree. He did smirk, but it was a bitter smirk paired with a shake of his head. "No deal. Trade or nothing. Your choice."

Her choice. Aliza almost wished that he had given her none. It would have been easier that way. This didn't feel like the rush of power she experienced as a Master, it felt like a horrendous burden weighing down on her stomach.

She wanted to save Franz. She wanted to help him the way he had helped her. She wanted to let him and Amos meet again. She wanted to make sure that he wasn't Commanded. She wanted to make sure that the man her father loved had a chance to repent of his sins so that when her father died, he really would have Franz waiting for him.

But...

But Aliza still couldn't remember her mother's face or her father's voice, and that was Hitler's fault. And if she accepted Franz, she would lose N-1. Hitler, Heydrich, Goebbels, Goering, Himmler. She wouldn't even be able to venture into Zone N-1 as an Invader or she would risk Yonah killing her to retake Franz's Contract.

She would remain a Master, but the power would become a burden, a *responsibility*. She would no longer be able to go down into Hell and Command with reckless abandon since no doubt some of the Subjects in Franz's Zone were his friends and comrades. Torturing *them* could hurt Franz, make him all the more hesitant to repent.

She would no longer truly be a God. Her vengeance would morph into labor. She would be forced to be kind and merciful even to people who deserved pain.

And she would never be able to see Hitler's face contort in pain again. Never be able to hear Heydrich scream. And they had taken so much from her, and she hated them so, *so* much for that.

A battle went on in Aliza Auman's soul for a moment: between love and hatred, anger and affection.

Anger won.

"I'm not giving you Hitler's soul for one little SS man!" she snapped. "You can keep Keidel! I'm the God of Nazi-Land! You can't have that!"

Aliza wanted Yonah to get angry. She wanted him to get as angry as she was because he had backed her into a corner. Because he had forced her to choose, and choosing N-1 made Aliza feel the same horrible sensation that she had experienced when she had made Heidi cry.

But Yonah just sighed, pointed at the thatch, and said, "There's the door. You go have fun in your Zone. I'll be having fun in mine."

She wanted to punch him in the face because it felt like her stomach was on fire. Instead, Aliza did something worse and kicked at his manuscript, sending papers flying everywhere.

"Hey!" Yonah cried, frantically trying to collect and reorder his precious pages. Aliza grabbed one just to be cruel, tore it in two, and then fled, desperate to find a safe place where she could go down into the Zone and let out some steam.

▽

ALIZA AUMAN THE HUMAN HAD BEEN USED TO HEARING *NO* quite a bit. There was nothing she despised more. Aliza Auman the God of Nazi-Land had gotten used to only hearing it when she bothered to venture out of her little universe.

A God that was denied what they wanted was wont to be wrathful, and since she couldn't truly take out her anger on Yonah, she naturally ended up delving into Zone N-1 and tried to find satisfaction in tormenting her Subjects.

"The bastard! ***Stab yourself!***"

Heydrich let out a gag of pain as the girl forced him to thrust his blade into his own chest.

"The damn bastard! ***Take it out!***"

Heydrich removed the dagger, coughing up blood and whimpering. It was a pathetic sight that would have normally lifted Aliza's spirit, but she was reminded of her weakness and Yonah's ability to refuse, refuse, *refuse.*

It simply wasn't fair.

"As though I'd trade you assholes for *one* SS man. He knows that's not a fair deal! Won't even fight me for it! Damn coward!"

The Nazis, for their part, had very little clue why the girl was so frustrated. She had burst in, forced Hitler to skin himself a few times, and after she had lost interest in the dictator, she had directed her attention to Heydrich. Judging from the way she was screaming about 'Yonah,' they assumed that there was some sort of lovers' quarrel going on, especially since she also kept mentioning someone named 'Franz.'

The Nazis had no clue who that was, and they certainly didn't care. They were too busy helplessly kneeling on the ground and waiting for their turn after Aliza grew tired of making Heydrich stab himself with the Artifact.

Hitler, who had been fixed up and forced to kneel alongside his comrades, had noticed something: the God of Nazi-Land hadn't Commanded them to be silent. The others were quiet out of self-preservation, but Hitler still had control of his tongue.

"Asshole!" the Master snapped, and with a wave of her hand, Heydrich was healed before he could bleed out on the hardwood floor. Heydrich barely got an opportunity to gasp before he was forced once more to bury his own dagger in his spleen again. Heydrich coughed and yelped in pain, but Hitler realized that once the knife was buried in the Hangman's gut, his movements were no longer jerky and his eyes were not utterly consumed with agony.

Heydrich had fulfilled the Command, which meant that until the Master Commanded again, he was free.

Hitler saw his opportunity and seized it.

"You're a pathetic little Jew! A stupid, worthless little Jew girl! I hope every subhuman in your family went up in smoke!" the Führer snapped, and that did the trick. The God of Nazi-Land whirled about, her eyes glowing gold. Heydrich, still holding his knife in his gut, met Hitler's gaze behind the Master's back.

"Heydrich, stay there," the Master Commanded. If Aliza had not been so consumed with anger, then she would have been more careful. She would have caught her mistake as quickly as Heydrich did: she had said *stay there.* She had not said: *freeze, don't move.*

She had not said: *don't take the knife out of your spleen.*

She had not said: *don't throw it at me.*

And single-minded Aliza did not realize her error, so

distracted was she by the steely-eyed Führer who now, for once, even as he trembled and kneeled, was acting like the Hitler that she had known. Not a frightened, pathetic little man, but a monster that was stupid and arrogant enough to insult a God.

Aliza was distracted by thoughts of exactly how she was going to make Hitler pay for that, and so she didn't hear a *squick* as Heydrich pulled his dagger from his own spleen, and it wasn't until the dagger was buried in her back that she realized what had happened.

There was pain only for a moment. Then, coldness, a suffocating coldness like she was being wrapped in a blanket made of snow. She felt her entire being go numb. She felt icicles invade her mind. She felt something inside her strain and strain, but whatever it was did not break.

She felt long after that. Anger and confusion and desperation like a drowning girl. But there was little she could do about it as she faded into darkness.

THE SUBJECTS HAD NEVER SEEN A MASTER DIE BEFORE. When this one did, this Master Six, it was strange. There was a flash of golden light, and the entire universe seemed to shudder. The Master's body was consumed by shadows, and then...static, her form shifting suddenly like the image on a poorly recorded film.

Then, she was gone, and there was only black ash blowing about the room. The dagger clattered to the ground.

"It...worked..." Hitler muttered, reaching out and grasping the SS dagger by the handle. Heydrich, still sporting a wound in his spleen, was unable to celebrate his victory as he collapsed to his side, coughing up blood. The other Subjects, freed of the Command that had forced them to kneel, unleashed sighs of relief.

"Reinhard!" Himmler cried, stumbling to his feet and running to his former subordinate. "Well done!"

Heydrich's only response to that remark was to grunt and spit up more blood, which made Himmler wince. Goering collapsed onto he nearest couch, panting as though he'd just been forced to walk up a three-story staircase. Goebbels ran to Hitler's side as the Führer examined the dagger.

"Brilliant, my Führer, simply brilliant!" the propagandist cried. "You were entirely correct!"

"Of course I was," Hitler mumbled, turning the blade over and examining the blood covering the gothic engraving.

"Oh, dear...where did the Contract go?" Goebbels noted, looking about the ash-covered floor and grimacing when he realized that the little golden triangle had vanished with the God of Nazi-Land.

"M-Maybe it's gone for good? Are we free now?" Himmler suggested hopefully, pressing a cushion from one of the couches against Heydrich's wound as the Hangman passed out from blood loss.

"I doubt it will be that easy." Hitler declared. "We'll likely get a break, and then another one will come just like last time."

Rising to his feet, Hitler quickly wiped the blade off on his brown uniform and twirled it in his hand, smiling for the first time since he had been damned.

"But," Hitler said, gesturing to the unconscious Hangman. "At least now we have a way to fight back."

Amos liked to give his daughters their privacy. He rarely ventured past the curtain in Heidi and Aliza's bedroom, and if they were gone for most of the day, he didn't question it unless they gave him a reason to. When Aliza stayed in her room all day, he assumed that she was in her Zone and left her be.

However, Amos hated wasting food, having lived through a time when so many people lost their lives to starvation. Thus, Amos never tolerated his daughters missing dinner without checking in first to make sure that he didn't make too much and waste their portion.

So when dinner was served and every Auman girl except Aliza came down, Amos sent Uta to retrieve her sister. Uta returned, reporting that Aliza was asleep.

"Shake her awake, then. She can't miss dinner," Amos said, and Uta shrugged.

"I did," the child declared. "She didn't wake up, but she's not dead 'cause I saw her breathing."

That made Amos lift an eyebrow: if Uta had so much as touched Aliza, that should have been enough to yank her out of the Zone.

"Must just be…really sleepy, then…" Amos muttered. That wasn't in and of itself surprising, he supposed: Aliza had been acting as his therapist just the other day, and that must have been truly tiring.

"Heidi," Amos begged. "I really don't wanna burst in on your sister. Mind going up and punching her a few times to wake her up?"

"Punch her?" Heidi said with a small smirk. "Gladly."

"Light punching only!" Amos ordered as Heidi bolted up the stairs, eager for some paternally sanctioned revenge. He expected to hear Aliza and Heidi screeching at one another, but after a few minutes, Heidi returned, pale-faced, concern pouring from her blue eyes.

"Dad…I really shook her, and she's not waking up,"

Heidi stuttered. "I...I mean she looks fine, like she's sleeping, but she's not...should I call someone?"

Amos felt his heart drop to the bottom of his stomach, where it remained for a few moments before leaping up into his throat, pounding frantically. "Y-yeah, call the doctor and watch your sisters."

Leaving Heidi to phone the hospital and calm the anxious younger girls, Amos ran to his daughters' room, parting Aliza's black curtain. There she was, lying down on her side, eyes closed, chest rising and falling in a steady rhythm. Aliza looked like she was simply sleeping peacefully, but indeed, when her father shook her, she didn't even stir.

"Aliza! Aliza!" Amos cried, and as he shook her, he looked down and realized that the Contract was missing from above her heart. Letting out a small gasp, Amos touched his own Contract, dread building as he curled up on the end of her bed and dove down into his own Zone.

He landed on his silver throne and leapt up, running to the Looking Glass and drawing "Zone N-1" into the mist, his hands trembling so terribly that they could barely write legibly.

His pounding heart somehow beat faster when the mist didn't clear, offering a way into Aliza's Zone. Instead, his writing vanished and was replaced with a golden script:

Unable to Accept. New Master Selection in Process for Zone: N-1.

"What?!" sputtered Amos in horrified disbelief. He wiped the message away with his hand and tried thrice more only to get the same response again and again.

"But she has to be in the Zone!" he cried, ramming his fist on the glass and for once feeling utterly and completely helpless in the midst of his own Zone. "Let me in, come on! Let me in! Aliza! Aliza! ALIZA!"

Ha-Satan was a busy Archangel. Such was to be expected of God's favorite, an angel that was at once a lawyer and the warden of the universe's largest prison: it was his task not only to compile the sins of the recently deceased, but to ensure that the long dead entrusted into his 'care' continued to receive their dues. Even with all the time in the world, he rarely paused.

Yet even he, busy Archangel that he was, stopped for a moment when a golden light flashed beside him as he worked at his desk, taking notes for his next trial. He turned his covered face towards several piles of golden triangles piled high on his workspace: yet to be assigned Contracts. Another one had been added to the pile. Ha-Satan set his pen down and picked it up, unfolding it.

If the Archangel had eyebrows, he would have raised them. Zone N-1's Contract had been returned to him, its signature line blank. If Aliza Auman had renounced the Contract, then it wouldn't have returned to Ha-Satan's desk: it would have remained on Earth until either a new Master found it and signed it, or Ha-Satan was notified that Nazi-Land needed a Master and sent a Cherub to collect it.

The Contract should have only returned this quickly for one reason: because the Master had died. Aliza Auman had been young, and in good health, and in a safe area. And besides, Ha-Satan and the Angel of Death were close co-workers, and they had long ago agreed for the sake of reducing Ha-Satan's workload that Masters would be the last to die of disease or old age.

Had Aliza Auman been murdered, then? Possibly, but Ha-Satan kept close tabs on the sins of man, and he hadn't been informed of any murders in Beth-Hadasha. Besides, he had just spoken with the Angel of Death moments ago so that he could know who would be facing Judgement soon, and Death had said nothing about Aliza Auman.

In a few hours, when he would speak to the Angel of Death, when his co-worker would assure him that Aliza Auman's soul had not been collected, Ha-Satan's curious concern would morph into dread as he realized that something had gone terribly, terribly wrong.

But right then, all he could do was sigh, decide that perhaps the Bureaucracy of Heaven had simply been tardy on the updates again, and proclaim, "What a shame…she had so much promise…oh, well…"

The Archangel folded the Contract back into a triangle and rose from his onyx desk. "On to the next one."

------------ ▽ ------------

To be continued in *The God of Nazi-Land*

Historical Notes

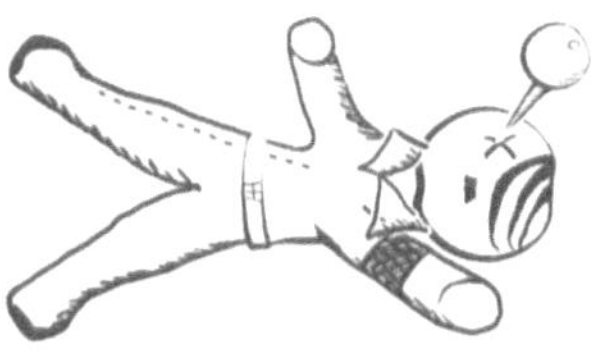

While *Aliza in Nazi-Land* is a work of historical fantasy, some of the plot points mentioned in this book are based on real life.

The Neo-Nazi march on Beth-Hadasha is based on the infamous case of *Village of Skokie v. Nat'l Socialist Party of America*. In 1978, Frank Collin's National Socialist Party of America declared that they intended to march through the village of Skokie.[1]

Given that Skokie was heavily Jewish and given that one sixth of the Jews living there were survivors of the Holocaust, the prospect of a Nazi march was considered provocative, and the Jewish citizens desperately set about trying to stop the Nazis.[2]

---

1. Strum, P. (1999). *When the Nazis Came to Skokie (Landmark Law Cases & American Society)*. Univ Pr of Kansas.
2. Strum, P. (1999). *When the Nazis Came to Skokie (Landmark Law Cases & American Society)*. Univ Pr of Kansas.

This led to an extensive and controversial legal battle which made it all the way to the Supreme Court.[3]

The Supreme Court ultimately decreed that the Neo-Nazis had the constitutional right to march, stating that, "The display of the swastika, as offensive to the principles of a free nation and the memories it recalls may be, is symbolic political speech intended to convey to the public the beliefs of those who display it."[4] Thus, the Nazis were given permission to march on Skokie with their swastikas. The National Socialists of America, however, ultimately never marched through Skokie, instead taking their rally to the Federal Plaza in downtown Chicago.[5]

When the American Nazi Party attempted to march through Skokie, they found themselves assisted by a strange ally: the American Civil Liberties Union ("ACLU"), and more specifically by a Jewish ACLU lawyer named David Goldberger.[6] The impact on the ACLU was severe. "Resignations began to pour in from all over the country immediately after news coverage of the Supreme Court decision in the case," wrote Goldberger years later, and indeed, the ACLU lost over 30,000 members over the Skokie debacle.[7]

Despite this, Goldberger found support from many members of the Jewish community, even those who had personally experienced the horrors of the Holocaust. "There were times when, during speeches I gave about the Skokie case, Holocaust survivors courageously stood up to

---

3. *Village of Skokie v. Nat'l Socialist Party of America*, 69 Ill.2d 605, 373 N.E.2d 21 (1978).
4. *Id.*
5. Strum, P. (1999). *When the Nazis Came to Skokie (Landmark Law Cases & American Society)*. Univ Pr of Kansas.
6. Strum, P. (1999). *When the Nazis Came to Skokie (Landmark Law Cases & American Society)*. Univ Pr of Kansas.
7. *Id.*

say that I was right to have represented the Nazis," Goldberger wrote, "These survivors said that they did not want the Nazis driven underground by speech-repressive laws or court injunctions. They explained that they wanted to be able to see their enemies in plain sight so they would know who they were."[8]

Goldberger would himself defend the ACLU's choice to represent the Nazis, noting that the ACLU had used similar arguments to defend Civil Rights Protestors in Southern states, where the states and cities had also tried to shut down protests under the pretense of preventing disruption of the peace. "No matter how offensive our clients are," proclaimed Goldberger, "chipping away at this commitment [to freedom of speech] will open the door to the erosion of the First Amendment as a bulwark against rule by tyrants."

Regarding the story that Yonah tells about Heydrich putting on the Czech crown: on November 19th of 1941, shortly after becoming the *Reichsprotektor* of occupied Czechoslovakia, Reinhard Heydrich was filmed examining the crown of Saint Wenceslaus. The crown, fashioned of gold and 921 precious jewels, was indeed said to be afflicted by a curse which stated that any usurper who placed it upon his head would die within the year, as well as his firstborn son.

A rumor was spread that Heydrich had placed the crown upon his head shortly after being pictured with it as a way of insulting the Czech people he ruled over, and this led to the rumor that his assassination, which occurred within the year, and the death of his firstborn son, Klaus, which occurred a year after, came about because of this. There is, however, no evidence that Heydrich actually did

---

8. *Id.*

place the crown upon his head, and while many historians dispute the story, it would be in his character to do so.

Concerning the death of Reinhard Heydrich's eldest son: Reinhard Klaus Heydrich, usually simply referred to as Klaus Heydrich, did die on October 24th of 1943, roughly a year after his father's death. The exact circumstances of his death are somewhat unclear. Klaus' younger brother Heider testified that, "Klaus was riding his bike and I was hanging on to the back of it when the car crashed into us, just outside the gate to our home. Klaus was killed but I was uninjured."

Some others, however, including Heydrich's wife Lina and a former house servant Helena Vovosa, have testified that Klaus alone biked outside the gate, which had been left open in order to accommodate a guest that was coming to visit—either Richard Hildebrandt or Heinrich Himmler himself, depending on the testimony. The gate which Klaus exited from leads into a sharp bend which would make it difficult for an incoming car to see anyone in the street (the author, who visited the Heydrichs' manor, can testify to almost being hit by a car herself.)

A Czech bus driver for the local football team, Karel Kasparov, ended up striking the boy with his vehicle. While he was arrested for this, he was ultimately released when the Nazi authorities determined that Klaus' own behavior caused the accident.

After being struck by the car, Klaus was tended to by a Jewish doctor from the prison detail working on the Heydrichs' property, however, nothing helped, and the ten-year-old died thirty minutes after the accident. Heinrich Himmler, who was Klaus' godfather, was reportedly very shaken by the child's death, and ended up flying to Prague to personally attend the boy's funeral.

A note to my readers

Thank you for reading! If you enjoyed this book, please tell your friends. I'd love to hear your thoughts on *The Hangman's Master*, and reviews help authors a great deal, so I'd be very grateful if you would post a short review on Amazon and/or Goodreads. If you'd like to read more stories like this and get notifications about free and discounted books and short stories, follow me on Facebook, Amazon, and sign up for my newsletter at elysehoffman.com! You can also follow me on Bookbub!

www.ingramcontent.com/pod-product-compliance
Lightning Source LLC
Chambersburg PA
CBHW021713190726
48289CB00008B/2509